Alias
Madame Doubtfire

Alias
Madame Doubtfire

Anne Fine

Joy Street Books
Little, Brown and Company
Boston   Toronto

First U.S. Edition

The characters and events in this book
are fictitious. Any similarities to real
persons, living or dead, are coincidental
and not intended by the author.

Library of Congress Cataloging-in-Publication Data
Fine, Anne.
    Alias Madame Doubtfire / by Anne Fine. — 1st U.S. ed.
        p.   cm.
    Summary: Miranda's three children thoroughly enjoy
their huge, overdressed baby-sitter/cleaning woman who is
actually their father in disguise, and they dread the day
when their mother discovers Madame Doubtfire is really
her ex-husband.
    ISBN 0-316-28313-4
    [1. Family life — Fiction.   2. Sex role — Fiction.
3. Divorce — Fiction.]   I. Title.
PZ7.F495673A1 1987
[Fic] — dc19   87-30195
                                                              CIP
                                                              AC

10 9 8 7 6 5 4 3 2 1

VB

Printed in the United States of America

For Tom and Fran

Alias
Madame Doubtfire

1

A Quiet Afternoon Tea with Father

All the way up the stairs, the children fought not to carry the envelope. Toward the top, Lydia took advantage of her height to force it down Christopher's sweater. Christopher pulled it out and tried to thrust it into Natalie's hand.

"Here, Natty," he said. "Give this to Dad."

Natalie shook her head so violently her hair whipped her cheeks pink. She interlaced her fingers behind her back. So Christopher tucked the envelope down the top of her pinafore dress, behind the yellow felt ducklings. Natalie's eyes filled with tears, and by the time Daniel Hilliard opened the door to let his children in, she was weeping gently.

He reached down to pick her up in his arms.

"Why do you always have to make her cry?" he asked the other two.

Lydia looked away. Christopher blushed.

"Sorry," they said.

Daniel carried Natalie through the hall into the kitchen and sat her on the edge of the table. Hearing a soft crumpling of paper inside her dress, he reached in behind the yellow felt ducklings, and pulled out the letter.

"Aha!" he cried. "Another missive from The Poison Pen. How *is* your mother, anyway?"

"Very well, thank you," Lydia informed him with slightly chilly courtesy.

"I'm very glad to hear it," he said. "I wouldn't like to think of her coming down with amoebic dysentery, or salmonella, or shingles." His eyes began to glitter. A little smile warped his lips. "Or Lassa fever, or rabies, or — "

"She had the beginnings of a slight cold last week," Lydia interrupted her father. "But it never got serious."

"Pity," said Daniel. "I mean, what a pity."

No one responded. Christopher had dropped on to his heels in front of the quail's cage, and was whistling to it through the bars. The tiny, silver-gray, feathery ball jumped up and down, peeping with excitement. Lydia was leafing curiously through the heaps of paperwork cluttering the table.

Natalie said:

"Daddy, Mother sent you her love."

"Did she?" Daniel was astonished. "Did she really?"

"No," Christopher said, reaching inside the cage to touch his pet.

"Of course not," said Lydia. "Natalie just made that up, or saw it on television or something."

Daniel scooped up his small daughter and gave her a squeeze.

"Oh, Natty," he said. "It's hard for you sometimes, isn't it?"

Natalie buried her face in his armpit.

"It might be easier for her," Lydia remarked, "if you yourself were to make a bit more of an effort."

Daniel peered sharply at his elder daughter over the hedge of Natalie's hair.

"What do you mean by that?"

"I mean," said Lydia, "that we are only here on Tuesdays for tea and every other weekend. It isn't much. So it would be quite nice if Natty didn't have to spend it listening to unpleasant remarks."

"Unpleasant remarks?" Embarrassed, Daniel feigned mystification.

"You know," said Lydia. " 'The Poison Pen,' all those diseases . . ."

"You're right," said Daniel. "You're quite right. I'll make more of an effort. I'll start now." He drew a breath. "I'm glad your mother's well. I'm pleased to hear it." He paused a moment. "I won't read her letter right this minute in case I change my mind about that. I'll put it up here on the shelf, and read it later."

He tucked the letter away between the cocoa and a large bag of quail food, and stood glowering at it for a moment. Then he turned back to his children.

"I expect it's only about remembering to take your coats home with you this time, or something like that."

Lydia and Christopher glanced at one another. They knew better. They'd read it. Indeed, they always read their mother's letters to their father. It came under their general heading of "self-defense." They even had a system. Lydia tore open the sealed envelope and took out the note. The two of them read it together, silently. Then Christopher would refold it in to the same creases as before, and slide it in a fresh envelope he'd taken from the packet in the desk. He'd carry it over to Natalie, who usually unthinkingly and obediently stuck out her tongue to lick the glue along the flap. This way they shared all the responsibility among the three of them and, with luck if they were ever caught, all the blame, too.

"It's sure to be the coats," Daniel repeated, entirely unconvinced. He scowled at the envelope again.

"Maybe," said Lydia. "She did mention quite a few times during the week how very inconvenient it was, not having our coats."

Daniel was irritated.

"You have other coats. You have the coats I bought you last winter."

The children were silent, and Daniel noticed.

"She doesn't like them, does she?" he said.

Trying to head him off, Lydia asked: "Could we have tea now? We're really quite hungry."

"The coats," Daniel insisted. "The coats. The coats I bought you last winter, at hideous expense. You never wear them over here. In fact, I've never seen you wearing them." The skin around his eyes was darkening to a thin glaze. The children looked away. They knew the signs. "You don't wear them, do you? No, you don't. She doesn't like them, so you're not allowed to wear them."

"I wear mine," Natalie offered. "I did wear mine on bonfire night, *and* when we went sledding, *and* when the park was all flooded and muddy, *and* when we slid down that hill in cardboard boxes, and Mother thought that there might be dog doo."

"See?" Daniel crowed triumphantly. "See? She only lets you wear my coats when she's afraid the coats *she* bought will get scorched, or ripped, or filthy, or — " (thinking of dog doo) " — worse."

The taut gray look around his eyes intensified, and seemingly without even noticing what he was doing, he lifted an imaginary rifle down from an imaginary rifle rack on the wall and, tilting his head slightly to one side, took imaginary aim through imaginary sights.

"What are you doing?" Lydia asked him. "Have you got a cramp in your neck?"

Embarrassed, Daniel made to hang the weapon back on the rack before, even more embarrassed, he came to his senses. To pull himself together, he squared his shoulders and breathed in deeply. The warm and comforting aroma of herbs and garlic filled his nostrils.

"The stuffed bread!" he remembered. "Ready to eat?"

"You bet!"

"Yes."

"Goody!"

They sprang to life. Using the side of her arm, Lydia bulldozed the untidy pile of all her father's most recent job applications farther along the table top, clearing a space. Christopher quickly fished through the cluttered drain board, searching for enough clean plates and silverware to get the four of them through the meal. Carefully, Natalie put out glasses and a carton of milk.

Cursing the steam that rose in his eyes and his scorched fingers, Daniel tipped the hot loaf out of the baking tin onto a serving dish, where it lay swollen and steaming for several seconds before it collapsed.

"Oh!"

"Nearly perfect!"

"Mother says that often happens if you cook it too long."

"I didn't *cook* it too long," he informed them. "It *waited* too long. Like me, it waited forty minutes until your mother was good enough to drop you off."

At this fresh criticism of her mother, Lydia tightened her lips.

"She said the traffic was bad."

Daniel tightened his.

"Naturally, the traffic patterns of her own home town would take your mother entirely by surprise. She's only lived here thirty-five years. She's only been a car driver for half of them. She's only driven you here at this time every Tuesday for the last couple of years. Naturally, she is as a stranger to the wheel, and the density of traffic astonishes her."

Lydia snapped:

"It isn't very easy for her, you know, being a single parent."

Daniel drew himself up.

"You don't need to tell *me*," he reminded her. "I am a single parent, too. And whereas she has you three to keep her company for most of the week, I don't. And you are forty minutes late, as usual. That's forty minutes off my time with you, my very limited time with you. Forty minutes shaved off yet again by her customary unpunctuality and lack of consideration for my feelings."

All three children had stopped chewing, but Daniel didn't notice. The same look as before was in his eyes; and, curling his lips into a hideous grimace, he reached into the drawer at the end of the table, and drew out an imaginary carving knife with one hand, while drawing the teapot toward him with the other. Still grinning horribly, he slowly and carefully drew the imaginary knife across the tea cosy's imaginary throat.

Christopher sighed. Natalie's lower lip stuck out, as if she might burst into tears.

"Oh, do stop being so silly!" Lydia scolded her father impatiently. "You're almost making Natty cry. You tell us off for it, and then you do exactly the same." She turned on her sister. "Now just stop being such a baby, Natty. He hasn't hurt the tea cosy. Or Mother. He just gets annoyed. He can't control himself. You're simply going to have to learn to ignore him."

"She's right," Daniel pitched in, filled with remorse. "Your sister's absolutely right. I can't control myself." He fell on his knees in front of Natalie's chair. "You're simply going to have to learn to ignore me."

"Fat chance," sighed Christopher.

"Fat chance," repeated Natalie. She patted her father's thin patch, and felt rather proud. "Fat chance," she said again, adding as a civil afterthought: "You can get up now."

"Thank you," said Daniel. He rose, brushing patches of grime from the floor off his trouser knees. "I promise I'll be better in the future. I'll practice all the rest of today, and be absolutely perfect by the time your mother drops you off here on Friday."

Lydia and Christopher froze. Natalie noticed at once. Her spoon drifted to a halt midway between her plate and her mouth, and she peered anxiously, first into Lydia's face, then into Christopher's, her eyes seeming both to widen and become glossier, until a huge tear gathered on each lower lid, swelling and trembling, threatening to spill.

Daniel whipped a purple-spotted handkerchief from his pocket and handed it to his daughter across the table. Natalie buried her face in its folds. Her father reached out for her, and she climbed into his lap, sobbing quietly. He wrapped his arms around her, and tucked her head in neatly under his chin. Over it, he said to the others with steely courtesy:

"No problem with the weekend, I hope? You are coming on Friday? I haven't made any mistake with the schedule, have I? It is my turn to have you for the weekend?"

Lydia smoothed out her face until it showed no expression whatsoever; but Christopher squirmed painfully in his chair. His eyes slid from his father's questioning look and involuntarily glanced up at the envelope still propped, unopened, against the bag of quail food.

And Daniel saw.

"Aha!"

In an instant, his good intentions dissolved. Bundling poor Natalie aside, he jumped to his feet, snatched down the envelope, and ripped it open. His eyes ran over the brief note, narrowing and flashing. His fingers gripped the paper's edge. His knuckles whitened.

"The witch! The selfish, thoughtless, inconsiderate witch!"

"Dad!"

"Robbing me of my weekends! How dare she? How *dare* she?"

"Dad, *please!*"

"I could murder her. Truly I could! Sometimes I think I could cheerfully slit her throat!"

"No! Daddy! No!" Natalie was off her chair in a moment. Tears scorching her cheeks, she hurled herself across the room, and beat him fiercely with her fists.

Lydia was shocked.

"Dad! Really! For God's sake!"

Christopher, hideously embarrassed, slid off his chair and crouched beside the quail's cage, out of the blast. He hated scenes. He reached out for the tiny, fat, gray, warm comfort of his pet, and wondered what Hetty had made of all these endless outbursts since the day he first carried her home from the pet shop. First, there were all those truly terrifying fights in the kitchen at the other house, when plates, and even food, went flying. Christopher, cowering with Lydia elsewhere in the house — often under Natalie's bed, where for some reason they felt safest — would hear the thuds and bangs and hysterically raised voices, and wonder if Hetty were safe behind her cage bars. What if his mother or father hurled something sharp, or narrow, or even just a little too hard? What if they crushed the bars, and Hetty? At calmer moments, Christopher begged to be allowed to move her cage up to his bedroom; but since he couldn't bring himself to explain why, for fear of setting one or another of his parents off again, his pleas were ignored.

So Hetty had to sit through all those awful, awful quarrels; and then the weeks and months of cold and grinding discussions about money and curtains and child support, and who would take which table, and who which photographs. Did all the arguments put her off her seed? Did they make her feel sick? And even now, ages after Dad had moved out to a place of his own and taken Hetty with him at Mother's suggestion, just when she might have been hoping for a quieter life in her old age, still there were these awful, unpredictable moments blowing up out of nowhere — no longer truly frightening, but still unpleasant and unsettling.

Did she mind? He hummed to Hetty in a soft and tuneless fashion as he ran his fingers over her feathers. It was the noise he always made when things around were turning nasty. It was like putting himself away behind a wall, and the sheer drab and insistent idiocy of the sound always worried Daniel terribly.

It worked. As soon as the unmusical drone penetrated Daniel's consciousness, he made a huge effort to rise above his bad temper, and consider the children.

Letting the note that had so enraged him drop to the floor, he pried Natalie away from his trouser legs, and carried her back to the kitchen table.

"Sorry," he said. "Slip of the tongue. Didn't really mean it. I promise I won't say nasty things about your mother again."

"Or say that you'll cheerfully slit her throat?"

"Or say that I'll cheerfully slit her throat."

Forcing herself to believe him, Natalie wiped her streaming eyes and nose across the sleeve of his jacket, leaving wide slug trails.

"Fat chance," she said bravely.

"That's my Natty."

"What's in the letter?"

"Never mind."

"Tell me."

"Not now."

"*Tell* me."

Daniel glanced at the elder two. Lydia had gone back to reading this week's pile of letters to various acting agencies, detailing his past successes and announcing his current availability. He was quite glad he had put out of sight all his handwritten notes to old friends in the theater, asking if they had heard on the grapevine of anything hopeful. Christopher, too, seemed absorbed, petting his quail. In fact, neither of the elder two appeared in the slightest bit interested in the contents of their mother's letter, and Daniel realized for the very first time that they must have worked out some way of getting access to them before he did. Wondering how, he explained to Natalie:

"Your mother thinks Lydia and Christopher need some new clothes. So she is keeping you all over Friday night, in order to take you shopping on Saturday morning. So you won't be getting to me until lunchtime."

"Teatime, more like," Christopher muttered bitterly; and when Lydia said nothing at all to defend her mother, he gathered up the courage to add: "It isn't fair. It *is* Dad's weekend. She didn't have to let buying clothes go until now. I only need socks, anyway. Dad can buy socks."

"I can indeed," Daniel assured him. "I can buy skirts, too. And gym shoes, and shorts, and even girls' underwear."

At this appalling rudeness, Natalie sniggered. Christopher burst into song.

"Anything she can buy, Dad can buy better!
"Dad can buy anything better than her!"

He held his hands out to Natalie, and swung her round in a circle, singing raucously. Natalie reached for her father as she swung past him, and made him join in, too. To Daniel's astonishment, Lydia joined in of her own accord.

"Anything she can buy, Dad can buy better!

"Dad can buy anything, better than her!"

"Yes, he can."

"Yes, I can."

"Yes, he can."

"Yes, I can."

"Yes, he can." "Yes, I can." "Yes, he can!"

They fell back, laughing, on the floor. Natalie climbed on her father's stomach and bounced up and down until, in self-defense, he pinned her down firmly.

Losing his head in all the excitement, Christopher shouted:

"Oh, go on! Tell her!"

Daniel let go of Natalie momentarily, in order to spread his hands.

"You know your mother . . . ," he warned gently.

"Phone her!"

"Tell her!"

"Why *should* we miss all Friday night with you, and most of Saturday?"

"You can buy socks!"

"It's only fair!"

"It's your weekend, not hers."

The voices, like the directives, gradually weakened. They, too, knew their mother.

"We could *ask.*"

"Yes, ask her!"

"She *might*. You never know."

"We could *suggest* it."

"Hint at it."

"She won't let us, though."

"She never does."

"Never!"

"It isn't *fair*, is it?"

"No, it's not fair . . ."

Daniel looked around at his children's faces, one raw with disappointment, two sourly miserable. He said to Lydia: "You knew when you came in here, didn't you?"

She nodded, too dispirited even to dissemble.

"You, too?"

Christopher shrugged.

"But Natalie didn't."

"She might as well have known," Christopher burst out. "It happens practically every time. Whenever it's our turn to come to you, Mother manages to find some excuse. Rakes up some old great-aunt who hasn't sent a present in years, but suddenly can't last another weekend without having tea with us."

"Or she buys tickets for something, and claims they only had seats left for that day."

"Or she makes sure we have to come home to go to the doctor."

"Or the dentist."

"Or the optician."

"Or we get to you hours late, because she's taking the car to be serviced."

"Or we get picked up hours early because she's fetching it back."

"We hardly ever see you."

"And when we do, she's on the phone all the time."

"Checking up on us, as if we were babies."

"Checking up on you."

In the next room the phone, like a timely haunting, began to ring. They sat, unnerved and silenced.

"I'll get it," Daniel said finally.

"Oh, no, you won't," said Lydia. "I can't stand any more today. *I'll* get it."

Fiercely, she pushed back the chair against which she'd been leaning. The noise it made scraping across the floor set all their teeth on edge. They sat without speaking as Lydia banged out through the kitchen door and lifted the receiver, to stop the phone's steady, insistent ringing. Daniel looked across at Natalie, who'd stuck her fingers in her ears. Gently, he pried them out, and kissed them. Christopher began his very unpleasant humming, but Daniel gritted his teeth and said nothing.

Lydia came back.

"Well?" Daniel teased. "Aren't you going to tell us what she said?"

It never occurred to him for a moment that she would. She never told. She'd walk back in scowling, but when you asked, she'd only shrug and say sulkily: "Nothing." She'd keep her peace for hours, sometimes forever, and only tell Daniel if she happened to catch him alone for a few moments rooting for flowerpots or hanging up laundry or coming out of the bathroom.

"That phone call . . ." she'd say, in a voice of stony detachment. Daniel would nod, to show he was paying attention. "She says your money came in four days late again this month, and please try to be a bit more punctual in the future." Or, "I'm to remind you that four socks that came with us a fortnight ago haven't turned up yet. Two matching brown, one long red, and a school one."

"Right-ho!" Daniel would say as cheerily as he could between clenched jaws. But Lydia would already have walked away.

It clearly wasn't anything quite so petty as socks this time, he suddenly realized. Her face was drawn and bloodless. She actually seemed to be swaying with rage. To his horror, he realized that this time, whatever it was her mother had rung up to say, it was so awful his daughter could not keep it to herself, even for a few moments. She was about to tell them all.

"Lydia!" he tried to stop her.

But it was too late. Already she had turned on

her brother, whose humming drone dried to a faint, dried, staccato crackle at the mere sight of the look on his sister's face.

"The message was for you," she told him. "It couldn't wait two hours till you got home. You had to be told now. She had to phone. You had to *know*."

"Know what?" he asked her, terrified.

She took a deep breath.

"Lydia! No!"

It was as if it were a taste so bad she had to spit it out at once.

"The cat got at your hamsters. This time he really got at them. He tore them up. They're dead, both of them, Henry and Madge. She says she walked into the house to see mess and gore spread all over the rug."

Her ghastly message unloaded, Lydia turned away in tears.

Christopher bent over where he sat, on the floor, and buried his head in his arms. His shoulders heaved.

Natalie's fingers crept back in her ears.

Daniel looked around at his pale, miserable family.

"Good old Miranda," he muttered softly to himself. "Another ruined teatime. So help me, one day I will slit her throat!"

But Natalie, with her fingers still crushed in her ears, didn't hear him.

2

Stark Naked in Front of the Neighbors

At six o'clock, Daniel realized he could no longer pretend he was waiting for the right moment to tell them his news. If he left it for very much longer, they would be gone. It would be four full days before they came again at the weekend, and at any time during those four days, any one of his children might hear his news from someone else.

He wanted to tell them himself. But on the other hand . . .

There was a bit of the gambler in Daniel Hilliard. Scouring the room for any excuse for a further postponement, his eyes fell on the quail, who appeared to be fast asleep in a corner of her cage.

When she next peeps, thought Daniel, I'll tell them my news. Definitely. No question.

He then sat very still indeed, fearing to startle Hetty into untimely wakefulness by any precipitous noise or gesture.

Christopher sneezed. The quail woke up and peeped.

That didn't count, Daniel assured himself.

Christopher sneezed again. He was sitting on the floor beside a pile of wood shavings spilled out on newspaper, gluing the largest and curliest of them into a convoluted grave marker which he intended to stick in the ground above the last remains of his hamsters. Each time he rooted through the heap in search of the perfect wood-shaving for the next spiralling flourish, a little cloud of dust rose up and tickled his nostrils. He sneezed a third time, even louder.

The quail peeped again. Knowing when he was beaten, Daniel rose to his feet, straightened his tie, cleared his throat loudly, and announced:

"I have some news."

Christopher looked up from his grave marker. Lydia peered at her father over the tattered comic book she was reading for the third time. Up at the table, Natalie stopped crayoning.

"I've got a job."

There was a moment's pause. Then Natalie giggled. The other two sucked in their cheeks and glanced at one another, but Daniel didn't notice. He was too embarrassed, telling the quail:

"Down at the Art College. Four mornings and two evenings a week."

By now, Natalie was hugging herself, and rocking gently. Christopher bent his head over his grave marker to conceal a smile, his first since the phone call. Lydia buried her face in her comic.

"It's not exactly a proper acting job," Daniel went on. "But it's not badly paid, not badly paid at all, considering . . ."

"Considering what?" asked Christopher, and Daniel answered a little hesitantly:

"Considering what I have to do."

Lydia asked slyly, "What *do* you have to do, Dad?"

Now it was Christopher's turn to giggle, and Natalie had to ram her fist into her mouth to keep from splurting with laughter. There was another short pause before Daniel answered airily, "Not very much. I just sort of sit about, really."

"Just sort of sit about?"

"Or stand about."

Lydia said, "And do you ever just sort of lie about, too?"

"I might just lie about, yes. Yes, I might, on occasion, if specially requested. Yes, I might."

Natalie could not contain herself any longer.

"What do you *wear*?" she called out. "Go on, Daddy, tell us! What do you *wear* to do this job?"

Flushing a rich, ruby color, Daniel accused his younger daughter:

"You knew! You knew already! You knew all the time!"

Christopher grinned.

"Mother's absolutely livid," he said with comfortable satisfaction. "She's totally wild. I've never, ever seen her so angry. Not when you terrified all the toddlers at Natalie's party, bursting in wearing that gorilla suit. Or when you pretended you had backed the car over Granny. Or even when you said you heard ticking coming from that shopping bag in Woolworth's, and the bomb disposal team blew up that old lady's groceries."

"I get your point," Daniel interrupted him coldly. "Your mother's not pleased."

"She certainly isn't."

"Well, maybe she should be. She's spent enough time recently, complaining that her money's late. Maybe she should be pleased that I have found myself a job at last."

"But, Dad!" cried Lydia. "*What* a job! Honestly! Nude modeling!"

Natalie couldn't help snickering.

"I don't have to be ashamed," Daniel insisted hotly. "It's a real job. It pays good money. *Somebody* has to do it." He drew himself up. "Indeed, I fancy I am rather good at it."

"So does Mrs. Hooper," Christopher told him.

Daniel stared.

"Mrs. Hooper? Mrs. Hooper who lives next door to you? How would she know?"

"She's seen you."

"*Seen* me?"

Daniel was horrified.

"Well, painted you, then."

"Painted me? What? Stark naked? With no clothes on?"

"So Mr. Hooper said, when he came around to Mother to complain."

"I don't *believe* it." Daniel clutched his head. "My own ex-next-door-neighbor seeing me stark naked!"

"She almost didn't believe it, either," said Lydia.

"She said she hardly recognized you at first with no clothes on, because you weren't a bit as she'd imagined."

"Imagined? *Imagined?*" Daniel went pale. "Do you mean to tell me that all those years when I was standing there in all innocence in my rubber boots, chatting to her over the fence about carrot root fly and potato blight, the woman was actually propped on her rake, imagining me without my clothes?"

"Well, that's what Mr. Hooper seems to think, because he came around complaining to Mother about it."

"He told Mother it was disgusting," Natalie reported happily.

"*Truly* disgusting," the others chimed. Clearly the

exact terms of the conversation were well embedded in their minds.

"Oh, did he?" said Daniel.

Without thinking, he lifted a few coils of imaginary rope from an imaginary heap on the floor, and idly started to tie a hangman's knot.

"And what," he asked in a dangerously casual voice, "did your dear mother have to say about that?"

Lydia and Christopher were both quick to frown at Natalie in a warning fashion. But not quite quick enough. Natalie told him:

"Mother said she thought it was disgusting, too."

Daniel pulled his imaginary hangman's knot a little bit tighter.

"Oh, did she?" he asked in glacial tones. "Oh, did she really?"

"Yes. Yes, she did."

"And then?" prompted Daniel, fingering his noose.

Not heeding any of the danger signs, Natalie prattled on into ever deeper water.

"Then Mr. Hooper took Mrs. Hooper's painting of you with no clothes on out of the grocery bag that he'd hidden it in to carry it over to our house, and he propped it up on the living-room table. Then he and Mother both stared at it for a little while. Then Mother started giggling."

"Did she, indeed?"

Natalie looked thoughtful.

"You don't often see Mother giggling," she remarked. "She's usually far too busy to giggle."

"Oh, yes, indeed," Daniel agreed. "Your mother is usually far too busy running the Empire to break off for a quick giggle. I'm honored that she saw fit to make an exception in this case."

"It isn't the Empire," Lydia defended her mother. "It's the Emporium. The Lighting Emporium. And you can't really blame her for giggling. Some parts of Mrs. Hooper's painting were very funny."

Daniel began to lash his imaginary rope to an overhead fitting.

"Oh, yes? Which parts, exactly, would those be?"

"*You* know," said Lydia, blushing a little in her turn. "The *funny* parts. You were stark naked!"

Daniel tested the strength of his imaginary rope, and checked that the slip worked well on his noose.

"Nude modeling is an honorable profession," he lectured them. "Art is worthwhile, and artists have to learn. If they learn most in what are commonly referred to as 'life classes,' then modeling for life classes is both an acceptable and a valuable contribution to a cultured and civilized society."

"Even without your clothes on?" Natalie giggled. She was trying to steer her father back as quickly as she could to that aspect of the topic that interested her most.

"Even without my clothes on," Daniel repeated gravely.

Christopher grinned.

"Then how come you didn't say hello?"

"I beg your pardon?"

"How come you didn't say hello to Mrs. Hooper at the art class? Three hours, she said, and you never so much as winked or nodded."

"I didn't *see* her!"

"She saw you, every bit of you. She says she was so close, she could have spat on your chest."

Daniel drew himself up to his full height, which was considerable.

"The woman's husband is quite right," he informed them. "She is disgusting, truly disgusting."

"She just thinks you could have been a little more neighborly. She told Mother: 'You never know, with people, do you? You live next door to them for years, and spend hours talking to them across the fence about silvery scurf and apple scab and soft rot. Suddenly you're sitting only a few feet away, and they don't even say hello!' "

"I didn't *see* her!"

"That's what Mother told her. Mother said you were probably so embarrassed about prancing around stark naked in front of perfect strangers that you couldn't look anyone in the eye."

Daniel gave his imaginary noose a very sharp tug.

"I was not 'prancing around,' " he informed them through gritted teeth. "I was standing quite still. I was 'Adam in the Garden.' "

"Mrs. Hooper says she always fancied that Adam had a bit more flesh on him than you do. She said she saw you more as 'The Grim Reaper.' "

Daniel glowered rather unpleasantly at all of his children.

"Mrs. Hooper is a Philistine," he told them. "So is her husband. So is your mother. Now do you have any further criticisms of me in my new employment you wish to relay, before we drop the topic once and for all?"

"There's no need to get mad at *us*," said Christopher. "Just because Mother disapproves of your new job."

"She doesn't disapprove of the *job*," insisted Lydia. "She says she quite understands that *somebody* has to model nude for people who happen to be studying art instead of going out and earning a sensible living. She simply says she can't for the life of her see why that somebody has to turn out to be her own children's father."

"In that case," said Daniel, "your mother is not only a Philistine, but a hypocrite, too. And not very sensible, either, since I will spend the money I earn paying her your child support a little more promptly."

"Mother says she doubts it. She says you won't earn very much anyway."

"Less in a week than our cleaning lady."

Daniel looked puzzled.

"But you don't have a cleaning lady."

"Not yet," Lydia conceded. "But we are getting one."

"What for? Why does your mother need a cleaning lady? Cleaning things is her hobby. Her house is spotless, flawless, perfect. It actually gleams at people when they walk in. It hurts their eyes. Surfaces keep winking and sparkling." He paused, remembering ancient battles, and added a little wistfully after a moment: "Still, that was the way she always liked it, wasn't it? Personally, I always found a little bit of clutter more comfortable."

He waved his arms about expansively, inviting them to enjoy all the comfortable clutter. The bookshelf in the corner that had fallen down at one end eight months before unfortunately caught his eye. So did the grubby paper lantern hanging in tatters from the lamp fitting. And the wastebasket that hadn't been emptied of apple cores, orange peel, and banana skins for so many weeks that it had formed the delusion that it was a little indoor compost heap, and had begun fermenting gently. Daniel's proud and proprietorial air gradually dwindled into a look of deepening unease. Thick layers of dust prevented any of his surfaces from even aspiring to gleam, let alone sparkle. The furniture was ill assorted and ill arranged. The blind hung awry. Discarded reading matter littered the room to such an extent that when, earlier, he'd ordered Christopher to keep his mess of wood shavings and glue on newspaper, his son had simply slid from the table onto the sea of color supplements all over the floor, and carried on.

The room, Daniel was forced to admit, was not far short of a hopelessly lost cause. Even Hetty had withdrawn cooperation from all attempts at good housekeeping, and kicked most of her stale food and soiled bedding out through the cage bars onto the floor.

Not for the first time since he became entirely responsible for his own domestic arrangements, Daniel felt a mild wave of depression sweep over him.

"This place could do with a bit of a spring clean," he admitted. "I should get down to it."

Merely the passing thought of all the hours of drudgery it would entail appalled him. To reinforce resolution, he turned to Lydia.

"Purely as a matter of interest, you understand," he began delicately, "and not wanting for one moment to pry into your mother's affairs — one unskilled laborer asking of another, as it were — how much will I be saving, cleaning my own home?"

"Three pounds an hour," Lydia answered him promptly.

"What?" Daniel was shocked. "Three pounds an hour? For cleaning an already immaculate house? For wiping the odd faint, accidental smear off the odd gleaming mirror? Are you quite sure?"

"The job does include child care," Lydia reminded her father.

"Child care?" Daniel was mystified.

"You know. Looking after all of us between the end of school and when Mother gets back home from work at half past six."

"You mean bothering to phone the police if one of you hasn't turned up by four thirty? Mentioning to your brother that he could hang up his blazer rather than leave it lying on the hall floor? Reminding Natty here when it's time for 'Sesame Street'? Supplying the odd spelling? Admiring the odd flourish of math? That sort of thing?"

"I suppose so."

"Three pounds an hour!" wailed Daniel. *"Three pounds an hour!* For little more than that I stand stiff as a garden rake in public, freezing my cluster to a prune!"

"There is a bit of light cooking," Lydia attempted to console him.

"Light cooking? Light cooking? Spreading the odd knife edge of peanut butter over the odd roll! Poaching an egg every now and again! Switching on the toaster! Some woman stands to earn three pounds an hour for that? I can't believe it! What can your mother be thinking of, to spend the money I send her this way?"

Lydia said frostily:

"It probably isn't *your* money. It's probably *hers*. She's earning more from The Emporium this year. And Mother thinks it's very poor economy to pay other people crummy wages — especially other women. She says you get a better job done if you don't exploit the fact that others pay less. She says it's this sort of expansive, managerial thinking that's got her where she is today — "

"The Undisputed Leader of the Empire!"

"Emp*orium*."

"Able to afford a cleaning lady, anyhow."

"Housekeeper, really," Christopher corrected him, and added carelessly: "Mother says her job involves a lot more traveling this year, and she'll need to leave us with someone dependable."

"Why can't she leave you with me? I am dependable. I'm also your father."

Christopher's expression changed. He suddenly looked drawn and tired. A little irritably, he answered:

"Because she can't."

"Can't?"

"Won't, then."

Daniel looked at him sharply.

"You asked her, did you? You suggested it?"

Christopher flushed. He was getting angry.

"Of *course* we suggested it," he retorted.

"And what did she say?"

"Not much," he answered flatly, and turned away.

Daniel took hold of his shoulders and turned him back.

"What — did — she — say?"

The others watched.

"She said that it would disrupt her routine."

"Disrupt her routine? *Disrupt her routine?*"

His son's face stayed expressionless.

Daniel curled one of his hands into a fist, and rammed it, hard, into the palm of the other.

"But you did want to come?" he pressed his son.

Christopher shook himself irritably, and turned to Lydia for help. She answered for him.

"Of *course* he wanted to come. So did I. So did Natty. Why should we want to stay there every afternoon with someone we don't even know, someone who's always saying: 'I'm not sure about that, dear. We'll just have to wait until your mother comes home, and then ask her.' We don't. We'd rather be around here with you. Much rather. But it isn't going to happen, is it? She's not going to let us, and I'm not going to cry about it!"

She suddenly looked as if she might, though.

Daniel said:

"I could ask her."

The children were silent.

"It's a reasonable request."

Still no one answered. Their faces, however, said plainly: since when has that made any difference?

Daniel considered.

"I could try taking your mother back to Court . . ."

Lydia shuddered.

"Oh, *please,* no! Not again! Not after last time! That was just horrible! *Horrible!*"

Hastily, Christopher came to his sister's support. "And it didn't work!"

"No," Daniel said. "It didn't work. She just started making up better excuses, and wasting even more of our time writing them down in her endless letters." The faraway, glazed look came into his eyes. "Have to try something else . . ."

He turned his back to his children, thinking hard, and drew his purple-spotted handkerchief from his pocket. Wrapping the corners of it around his fingers, he pulled it taut. Then, before he even realized what he'd done, he'd coiled the resulting short tether around the nearest object, a large sliced loaf of bread, and garotted it firmly.

Slices of bread burst out in every direction.

The children stared.

3

A Visit from the Witch

While they were still picking bits of bread off the floor, a car horn sounded in the street.

Daniel glanced surreptitiously at the wall clock. It was barely twenty minutes to seven. Irritated, he affected not to have heard the sharp summons.

Christopher rose to his feet and wiped the bread crumbs off his hands. Lydia looked at the mess still scattered on the floor, and hesitated. Natalie piped up:

"That must be Mother."

"*Surely* not!" Daniel pretended brisk disbelief. "It can't possibly be your mother. It's far too soon. At least twenty minutes too early." He tipped the remains of the ruined loaf into the garbage. "It must be someone else entirely."

Christopher moved close enough to the window to glance down at the street without being seen.

"Someone else with a Volvo?" he asked.

"Why not?"

Helplessly, Christopher looked across at Lydia, who raised her eyes to heaven, and sighed.

"A red one?" Christopher persisted.

"It happens. It is not unheard of," Daniel answered stubbornly. With false nonchalance he tossed the dustpan and brush back in the cupboard. "There's more than one red Volvo in this town."

"More than one with the back piled with Lighting Emporium boxes? More than one with a redheaded lady in the front, losing her temper?"

The car horn sounded a second time, harsh and peremptory.

"Dad —?" Natalie begged, her eyes filling with tears.

The car horn blared. Galvanized by the sheer impatience in the sound, the children began to race around the room, gathering their belongings.

"Stop!" Daniel shouted. "Stop running about like headless chickens! There's no need for this *panic!*"

They stopped in their tracks, hesitant and anxious. Daniel spread out his hands, and argued:

"She doesn't even know for certain you're up here. You're not due to be collected for twenty minutes. We might be at the store or in the park. She doesn't know."

"She knows," said Christopher. He picked up his coat and began struggling into it.

"Take off that coat!" roared Daniel.

Christopher stared.

"Take off that coat!"

Christopher peeled the rumpled sleeve from his arm, and hurled the coat down on the floor.

"You'll get us into trouble!" he yelled.

"You will," agreed Lydia.

"Please let us go, Daddy," pleaded Natalie.

"Listen to me," said Daniel. He took a deep breath and tried to keep calm. "Listen to me, all three of you. This can't go on. She drops you off here forty minutes late, and you don't dare say a word to her. She comes to pick you up twenty minutes early. She honks the horn, and suddenly not one of you can think of anything but scuttling obediently down there."

He pointed.

"Look at poor Natty! She's terrified already. Two minutes her mother's been waiting in the car, and Natalie's nearly in tears."

He pointed to himself.

"Look at me! I had to wait a whole week, and then an extra forty minutes. Nobody nearly burst into tears about that!"

"It's not the same," Christopher argued.

"Why not? Why *not?*"

"You know why not."

"I certainly do!" Their father's self-control was slipping, fast. "It's not the same because of that selfish, thoughtless, inconsiderate witch out there! That's why not, isn't it?"

He slammed the side of his hand down, hard, on the table.

"Now this can't go on. Do you understand? *It can't go on.* You're not just *her* children, you know. You're mine, too. She has no right to treat us this way. I was an adequate father." He drew himself up. "No, I'd go further than that. I was a very *good* father. I made sure she remembered her vitamin tablets when she was pregnant. I fed her good, wholesome food and made her stop smoking. I did all the heavy shopping, and cheered her up, and brought her endless cups of tea. And whenever she lost her nerve and said that the last thing in the world she wanted was a baby, I promised to take you to the nearest orphanage the moment you were born, and leave you on the doorstep in a box. What man could do more? Then, after each of you was born, I did my best. I fetched you, carried you, bathed you, changed your diapers, diced your food, untangled your mobiles, pushed your prams . . ."

He was in full blast. Lydia and Christopher stood in sullen silence, while Natalie looked weepy and confused.

"I've sat through as many boring old child health-care clinics and grisly play groups in church halls as she has, I assure you. I've frosted your birthday cakes, and wallpapered your bedrooms." He banged his chest. "I was even the damn tooth fairy! Oh, yes. Make no mistake, I did as much as she did. You are my children as much as hers!"

Lydia and Christopher glowered, deeply indignant at the lecture, and smarting particularly under its implications of ownership. Natalie stood with her eyes lowered, inspecting her thumbs. She hadn't realized that before, about the tooth fairy . . .

Sensing their growing resentment at his harangue, Daniel made a massive effort to lower his voice to a tolerable level.

"Now what are we going to do about this?" he demanded. "What are we to do? I've offered to go back to Court to try to stop her carving hours off what was agreed to be my time with you. You all said no. You couldn't say no quickly enough. Well, that's all right. It's your decision, and I can't say I blame you."

He spread his hands, pleading.

"But what about me? Where does this leave me? Nowhere, that's where. And I can't stand that any longer."

He peered at each of his children in turn, scoured Lydia's deadpan face and Christopher's defensive scowl, then the troubled, tearful look of his youngest.

"So," he wound up. "If you three won't allow me to ask the Court to stand up to your mother for you, there's only one thing to do. You'll have to learn to stand up to her yourselves."

The children stared at him, simply appalled.

"What else can be done?" he asked softly. "Tell me. I'd love to know. What alternative is there to you three learning to stand up to her?"

In a flash, Christopher replied:

"You could stand up to her yourself!"

Now it was Daniel's turn to show dismay.

"Who? *Me?*"

"Yes. You. You're quick enough to tell us to do it. You do it first."

"All right," cried Daniel. "All right, I will!" Inspired by his own eloquence, he found he had the courage of Jove. Laying his arm across his son's shoulders, he assured him with confidence: "You are *on,* Buster! You are definitely on! Just stay and watch me!"

Just at that moment, out in the hall, they heard a demented rattling. It was followed by an enormous bang as the front door swung open and hit the wall. The sound of ceiling plaster slithering down the walls filled a brief and astonished moment.

"Mother!"

"She's come up!"

"Fed up with waiting in the car!"

"Oh, Christ!" muttered Daniel, all his declared valor shrinking into pure funk on the spot.

As the high heels tapped closer down the hall, Christopher seized the opportunity to exact sweet revenge on his father for subjecting them all to his fiery tirade.

"Now, Dad," he whispered, squeezing his arm and lifting a face that glowed with happy and innocent expectation. "Stand *up* to her. Don't let us down."

Miranda Hilliard, managing director of Hilliard's Lighting Emporium, appeared in the doorway. She was dressed smartly from top to toe in glossy black and purest white. Her thick and luscious hair, piled high on her head, was held in place by one small and strategically placed diamanté clip. In her three-inch heels, she was taller than Daniel.

"Good evening, Dan."

"Evening, Miranda."

"Your front door's a little bit sticky."

"It was locked."

"Oh, was it?" She glanced back over her shoulder along the hall at the hole freshly gouged in the wallpaper by the door handle, and the flakes of ceiling plaster sprinkled all over the floorboards.

"Well, never mind," she offered vaguely.

"No, never mind," Daniel agreed, as pleasantly as he could. But she'd lost interest anyway. Already she was gazing around the room, sizing up dangers:

frayed electrical wires trailing across the floors, a pair of garden shears lying, open-jawed, on a stool at knee height; and taking in all the small details of disorder: what was piled on the surfaces, what was chipped or broken, what would have benefited from a thorough wiping.

"One of your burners not working properly?" she inquired, glancing toward the gas stove.

Before he could prevent himself, Daniel cried out in astonishment:

"How did you know?"

She shrugged.

"Obvious," she told him. "It's not quite so impacted with grease as the other three."

She stepped a little farther into the room, her skirt swinging. Atop her frilly blouse, she wore a skimpy velvet bodice that Daniel remembered with affection from the old days. It always intrigued him to see which items of her wardrobe he still recognized. His former wife had the capacity, he'd recently realized, to make her clothes last forever, and, in an unguarded moment, he'd made the mistake of telling her so. "It's called looking after them properly," she'd countered sharply. So Daniel no longer dared remark upon what she wore. But he noticed.

"What's this thing here?"

She was pointing inside the quail's cage.

"That? That is Hetty, Christopher's quail."

"Really? I don't remember it looking like that."

"It's wearing a different cage now," explained Daniel.

Miranda ignored this. She was regarding the quail with the deepest suspicion.

"Does it make very much mess? I can't remember."

"Not very much," Daniel defended Hetty. There was, he knew from past experience, no point in waiting for Christopher to speak up. All three children were in the habit of falling silent when both their parents were in the same room. It was almost as if they felt they no longer counted beside something larger, longer running, much more dangerous.

"There's plenty of mess on the floor by its cage."

"That's because I haven't swept that side of the kitchen for several days," Daniel confessed.

"Judging by all the bits of bread on the floor under the table, you haven't swept the other side for even longer."

Daniel tried hard to muster an agreeable smile. It surfaced as a contorted grimace.

Miranda poked her finger between the cage bars, and prodded the sleeping quail.

"Does it make noise?"

Daniel lifted an eyebrow.

"What do you mean, does it make noise? You

must remember what noise it makes. You lived with it for months. It peeps."

"Peeps?"

She prodded Hetty again, a little bit harder. Courteously and cooperatively, Hetty jumped up and down in her cage, and peeped.

"Is that the noise?"

"Yes," Daniel said. "That's the quail, peeping."

Miranda flicked wisps of soiled quail bedding off her skirt as she swung round.

"That's fine, then," she said. "We'll take it."

"Take what?"

"That quail."

"Listen," said Daniel. He could feel his son's accusing eyes on his back. "This is not a pet shop, Miranda. This is a home." He leaned his face closer to that of his former wife, and spoke to her very loudly and slowly, as if she were both hard of hearing and slow in wits. "A — *home*. Do — you — *understand* — me? *People* live here. *I* do for one. *And,* from time to time, *Christopher here,* for *another.* It is *his quail. You — cannot — buy — it.*"

A hint of pink rose in Miranda Hilliard's cheeks.

"Don't be so foolish, Daniel," she told him. "I don't want to buy it. I want to *take* it. I think it would be very nice for Christopher if there was something to put in the empty cage at home, to make up a little for his dead hamsters."

"And what do you suggest we put in this empty cage here," asked Daniel between clenched teeth, "to make up a little for his missing quail?"

Miranda shrugged her shoulders. The bodice lifted.

"Oh, heavens, Dan! Don't be so awkward. The poor boy's just lost his hamsters! Can't you stop standing on your rights for once, and try to be a tiny bit less selfish and thoughtless and inconsiderate?"

"Selfish and thoughtless and inconsiderate? *Me?*"

Daniel was outraged.

"And there's no need to make a big drama about it. I simply haven't the time to listen."

She turned to the children.

"Now gather up your things. We're in a hurry." She took an envelope from her handbag. "I have to drop this at the newspaper office on the way home."

"Is that the ad for the cleaning lady?" Lydia asked her mother. It was the first time any of the children had spoken since her arrival. It was a hint to Daniel, and he knew it. He was supposed to stand up to her now.

Unable to think of anything else to say, he asked:

"Can I read it?"

Miranda sounded surprised.

"If you like."

She handed the advertisement over. It was written on a printed newspaper coupon in the form of a grid. Inside the little blank rectangular boxes above the number of the credit card to be debited, Miranda had printed:

RELIABLE	NON-SMOKING	CLEANING	LADY
REQUIRED.	SOME	CHILD	CARE
DAILY	AFTER	SCHOOL.	OTHER
HOURS	NEGOTIABLE.	PHONE	43184
FOR	INTERVIEW.		

Before he had even read to the end, Christopher had snatched it, and Natalie was begging to be told what it said. Daniel finished reading over his son's shoulder. Then he realized Christopher had turned, and was looking up in his face with a beseeching expression reminiscent of some of the more anguished illustrations in Natalie's colorful *Best Bible Stories*. Lydia, on the other hand, was regarding him with a look that, to his dismay, might have been laced with cynicism.

Natalie's face was easy to interpret. It was brimful of hope. His younger daughter, at least, was banking on him.

He could not bring himself to let her down. He summoned all his reserves of courage.

"Miranda!" he began, bravely enough. "About this advertisement. You don't need to go to all this trouble and expense hiring a cleaning lady or a housekeeper. Why don't the children simply stop off here after school, and you can pick them up on your way home from work?"

Miranda was barely listening. She was cramming the large bag of quail food inside her handbag.

"I don't think so, thank you, Daniel," she said, adding indifferently after a moment: "Nice of you to offer, though."

"I'm not offering," explained Daniel gently. "I'm *asking*."

"Asking?"

The voice was frigid. Miranda's eyes were suddenly cold, hard, little snowballs. The temperature in the room seemed to have dropped several degrees.

"Asking?" she repeated, in frosted tones.

He tried to say: "Demanding," or even: "Insisting." He tried his hardest. But though he could feel the children's eyes on him as well as hers, he could not do it. It was, he thought in desperation, a bit like being in one of those cheap paperback books Christopher was always reading, where you have to make endless choices to build your own story.

Alone, you face the wicked witch. The peaceful little villagers have begged you to stand up to her on their behalf. They have been terrorized for years, and now stand round in little clumps, watching. But the witch transfixes you with her steely gaze.

"Asking?" she says.

Do you:

A: Answer in ringing tones: "No! Demanding! And I will tolerate no argument!" and turn to page 94 where the witch collapses, defeated. Or:

B: Answer weakly: "Well, hoping really . . ." and turn, defeated yourself, to page 104, where all the little villagers bow their heads in shame at your faintheartedness.

"Well, hoping really . . ."

Miranda snapped her handbag shut so fiercely that little jets of excess quail food sprayed out and ricocheted against the wall.

"I'll think about it," she said, in tones that made it crystal-clear she wouldn't.

Once again, Daniel felt all the failure, self-disgust, and despair that had shadowed him the morning he'd left home for good, and had made the mistake of turning at the garden gate to see three set, unsmiling faces watching him from an upstairs window. The same three faces watched him now. Their disappointment was intense. A glistening tear tracked slowly down Christopher's cheek, and dropped on the newspaper coupon, flooding and blurring the telephone number.

Christopher rarely cried, and this was the second time within hours that Daniel had seen tears on his son's face. Daniel felt terrible. He turned away, and, as he did so, his eyes fell on yet another of the letters he was writing so hopefully to all the actors' agencies he knew about, listing the parts he had successfully played on the stage, and asking if they had any likely openings.

An idea suddenly came to him — an idea of inordinate daring and brilliance.

"Here," he said hastily, reaching out for the coupon. "I'll fix that smudge for you."

Turning his back on all of them, he flattened out the coupon on the table.

"I'll paint it out with correction fluid," he said, reaching for the tiny white bottle. He unscrewed the brush top, and dabbed at the coupon. "There, that's better. And it's dry already. Now I'll just put your telephone number in again, shall I? Four-three-one-eight-four," he intoned carefully and clearly as he wrote on the freshly painted space in the grid, equally clearly and carefully: six-six-seven-one-six — his own number.

"There," he said triumphantly. "That's a lot better."

Before anyone could stop him, he had thrust the coupon into its envelope, licked the flap, pressed it down, and run his thumb along to seal it.

Natalie let out a little wail of disappointment. It was traditional that licking the flaps of envelopes was her job.

"Oh, sorry, Natty," Daniel apologized. "Not at all like me to forget you."

He turned to his former wife.

"Stamp, Miranda?"

"No, thanks." Miranda shook her head. "Christopher can hop out of the car and drop it through the newspaper office letter box as we go by."

"Right-ho," Daniel said cheerfully, patting his son on the back.

Angry and disappointed, Christopher stepped out of reach, and turned reproachful eyes on his father. *Traitor*, the look on his face said plainly. Then he turned to his mother, clearly about to try to do better himself.

"Mother!" His voice was petulant. "Why did we have to be picked up so early today?"

"Early?" Miranda glanced at the wall clock. "I don't know what you're talking about, Christopher. It's five past seven already. Now pick your coat up off the floor. Daniel, I wish you wouldn't let them leave their clothes lying about like this. Coats are expensive, you know."

She moved toward the door.

"You'll let us borrow the cage, won't you? Just to get the quail home."

"The quail *is* home," Christopher muttered with all the insolence of remaindered rebellion.

Miranda ignored him. So Christopher turned his back on her, and picked up his grave marker from the table.

"Leave that horrid mess of wood shavings and glue behind here, would you, darling?"

She looked around.

"I think that's everything. Well, goodbye, Daniel. The children will see you on Saturday morning. I'm not quite sure when, but just as soon as we have finished our shopping."

Daniel reached out his arms to each child in turn as they filed past. Christopher's hug was perfunctory. Lydia used Hetty's cage as a shield to protect herself from him. Even forgiving Natalie's hug was brief.

Daniel nodded coolly at Miranda as she herded them out, one by one. He waited until they had walked down the hall and left his apartment, shutting the door behind them, before he moved. Then he sprinted along the passage and swung the front door open again, so he could listen to their departing footsteps echoing in the high space of the stairwell.

The sound of clattering heels grew fainter. Daniel inspected his lock. The side that housed the dead bolt was hanging off. The whole thing would need unscrewing and replacing.

Daniel's eyes narrowed. Stealthily, he reached inside his shirt, and drew out an imaginary hand grenade. Pulling out the imaginary pin with his teeth, he waited only until he was quite sure his children had disappeared safely through the heavy main entrance door into the street before he hurled it, with all the force he could muster, down the stone stairwell after his former wife.

Then, satisfied, he leaned back against the ruined door. A smile of pleasure spread over his face, and, for the first time that afternoon, he seemed at peace.

He was listening to the imaginary explosion.

4

A Good Interview Technique Can Work Wonders

Miranda Hilliard expected to receive a lot more than four telephone calls in response to her advertisement in the *Chronicle & Echo*. But there could have been no mistake in the printing. She hadn't actually seen the advertisement herself: mysteriously, her evening paper was not lying in the porch as usual when she came home from work, and the newsagent on the corner could not sell her another.

"It always happens that way," he assured her. "The very day one of my regulars especially wants a copy, some long, thin fellow I've never even seen before dives in and buys the lot."

But the advertisement must have been printed

correctly, for there were the four enquiries. The first came just as Miranda was dishing up the evening meal. The caller's voice was high-pitched, hoarse even, as if the woman had a throat problem. It also sounded deeply suspicious.

"Children, you said. Children after school . . ."

"That's right," Miranda confirmed. "Three children."

"Three? That's a lot. What sort are they?"

"What sort?"

Miranda looked at them, baffled.

"Boys or girls?"

"Oh! Two girls and a boy."

There was a stony silence.

"Something wrong?" asked Miranda, a little unnerved.

The voice spun down the line, taut, high and querulous.

"Yes. Don't like girls. Sorry. Goodbye."

There was a click. Miranda stared at the receiver.

"Well!" she gasped. "Good thing we don't like you, either."

The second call, too, came while they were eating. No throat problems here. The voice was rich and mellifluous.

"Hello? Is this four-three-one-eight-four? The ad?"

"That's right, yes," said Miranda.

"Child care, you mentioned."

"Yes, just a little. After school."

"Girls, are they?"

"Yes, said Miranda, looking at Lydia and Natalie. "Two of the three. And the third is a boy."

"Oh, dear."

The voice rang with disappointment.

"Is there a problem?" asked Miranda.

"Oh, dear me, yes. Can't do with boys. No. Sorry."

The caller hung up. Miranda gritted her teeth.

"*I'm* not," she told the silent telephone.

The third call came only a few minutes later, over the apple tart.

" 'allo?"

"Hello?"

Miranda's voice was becoming wary, the children noticed.

" 'allo. I phone regarding the advertisement." This voice was soft and buttery and foreign. " 'ow many children?"

"Three. Two girls and one boy."

" 'ow old?"

Miranda began to rattle off their ages. Before she'd even worked her way as far around the table as Natalie, the woman had hung up.

"Too old," she'd said. "Don't care for old. Only care for little."

Miranda banged the receiver onto its cradle.

"No problem!" she snapped. "Don't care for you much, either."

The last call came three hours later, just as Miranda was wondering if it were hopeless. Milk for the bedtime cocoa was rising in the pan as the phone rang. Miranda flew at the stove to rescue the milk, then at the telephone, which mercifully kept ringing.

The voice at the other end was rumbling and cheerful, but a little bit muffled, as if the woman had just wiped her nose and not yet lowered her handkerchief to speak in the mouthpiece.

"I've been attached to the same children now for years and years. They do grow older, don't they? And now I find I have the time to think of taking on your little nestful during the afternoons."

Miranda said, without much optimism:

"I'm afraid I do have two girls . . ."

The voice replied in a somewhat bracing fashion:

"*Lovely,* dear. Girls are precious gems."

But Miranda was still apologetic.

"And there's a boy . . ."

"A boy! I don't need to see him to know he's a fine lad!"

Scarcely believing that her luck was holding, Miranda embarked on detailing their ages, only to find herself at once interrupted.

"All ages are the nicest, I say."

"A little light cooking . . ."

"Oh, dear."

There was a silence, during which Miranda could

hear her heart pounding. Then down the line came the anxious explanation.

"I really should warn you now, dear, I'll only feed them good, proper food. Snacks or meals, I don't mind. I do both. But it has to be nourishment I'm giving them, not rubbish. I don't hold with all these unwholesome new things in packets. And I won't budge on that, dear, however loud and long the little poppets squawk at me. Mind you, I've had very little trouble up till now, once they understood it was to be good food or empty little tummies."

Miranda's eyes widened. Could this treasure be real?

"No smoking . . ." she murmured hesitantly.

"A nasty habit. Makes the curtains smell."

"Reliable . . ."

"Not missed a day in years, pet," the voice claimed proudly.

Miranda stretched out a hand to steady herself against the kitchen wall.

"An interview, perhaps?"

"Certainly, dear. But I'm sure you're very busy all day at the office. How about tomorrow evening at seven thirty? Would that suit? Name, dear? Address?"

"Hilliard," Miranda said faintly. "Ten Springer Avenue."

"Right on my bus route."

Miranda tried pinching herself, to see if she were

dreaming. The last two baby-sitters had come, or regularly failed to come, in undependable old cars.

"That's perfect," she said. "We'll all look forward to meeting you tomorrow." She hesitated. "Mrs. . . . ? Ms. . . . ?"

"Madame, dear. Madame Doubtfire."

Miranda could not disguise her astonishment.

"*Madame Doubtfire?*"

"That's right, dear. Madame Doubtfire. You've got it."

"Madame Doubtfire," repeated Miranda. But the line had gone dead.

Miranda seemed reluctant to place the receiver back on the cradle in case the miracle should end with the call.

"Tomorrow at seven thirty," she repeated softly. "Madame Doubtfire. Perfect!"

And perfect she did seem to be. Natalie met her first. Hearing a soft knock as she was padding past the front door in her candy-striped pajamas on the way up to bed, she raised herself on tiptoes and lifted the latch.

A vast apparition towered over her on the doorstep. It wore a loose salmon pink coat, beneath which hung boldly patterned skirts that hid all but a few inches of dark green rubber boots. Its head was swathed in a bulging turban held together with numerous safety pins and a glittery turquoise brooch. Coils of feathery scarf floated around its neck, and tucked under its arm was an enormous imitation crocodile handbag.

"You must be little Natalie."

Natalie nodded, and stared at the apparition.

"I'm Madame Doubtfire, dear."

Natalie nodded again, wide-eyed. Underneath the great flowery turban, the eyelids were larded with mauve, the cheeks unnaturally pink, the lips bright scarlet.

"Going up to bed, are we?"

Natalie nodded a third time, still speechless.

A huge hand appeared from between the loose folds of coat, and took her own. The apparition stepped forward into the house. Natalie stepped back. One large green boot heel was raised sufficiently to push the front door back gently till it clicked shut.

"Come on, then. Up we go."

At the narrow turn in the staircase, Natalie was forced to drop the apparition's hand, and move in front. Reaching the top step, she felt a familiar tap on her bottom.

"Brushed your teeth, poppet?"

Natalie shook her head.

"The bathroom first, then."

Natalie padded obediently along to the bathroom. While she took her brush from its hedghog holder and squeezed on toothpaste and brushed her teeth, avoiding all the wobbly ones, the apparition sat on the edge of the bathtub and fretted about the plants on the window ledge.

"Don't like the look of those pinks. They've been drenched. I must talk to your mother about that tomorrow. Now don't let me forget, young Natalie. Pinks simply *hate* to get their feet wet."

Over her frenzied brushing, Natalie scrutinized the pinks for signs of misery, while the apparition focused attention on the climbers.

"That philodendron needs a thorough good feed. Look at it, pasty little runt. Oh, I can see I'll have my work cut out for me in this house."

Natalie confided through a mouthful of pink froth:

"There's plants in the kitchen with all dead leaves. Mother's very cross. She can't work out what's wrong with them."

"Perhaps they don't like the atmosphere . . ."

Natalie took longer than usual to rinse her toothbrush and shake it dry. In the mirror over the basin she was watching the reflection of the face behind her. The gaudily lidded eyes met hers in the glass.

"Ready for bed?"

Natalie nodded.

"Two minutes, then."

The door was shut, leaving her alone. Natalie tugged down her pajama bottoms and sat on the toilet seat, thinking. Then she reached out an experimental finger to prod the pinks' plant pot. The soil was sodden.

"Poor pinks," she said. "Hate getting their feet wet."

And, rinsing her hands, she took the greatest care not to splash any more water over the plants on the window ledge.

When she came in her bedroom, her bedcovers had been turned back, and her library books laid out invitingly on her pillow. Ignoring them, Natalie knelt by the bookcase and slid out from the bottom shelf a battered picture book she hadn't touched for over two years.

The Looking Glass River.

The book was read from first page to last, not one sentence skipped, not one silly question or interruption. Just the same old magical pictures, and the words exactly as she remembered.

Then the bedside lamp was switched off, and the room was in darkness. One slim bar of light flooded through the slightly open door, and lit a strip of the far wall.

"Good night. Sleep tight."

Natalie stretched out her arms and circled them around the apparition's neck, pulling it closer.

"Good night, Daddy."

The apparition took a moment to recover its composure. Then it said sternly:

"You won't say a word tomorrow, will you, Natty?"

But Natalie was already yawning hugely, half asleep.

"No, Daddy."

The apparition tore distractedly at its slipping turban.

"And don't you call me that! I'm Madame Doubtfire!"

"All right, Daddy."

"Madame Doubtfire!"

"All right, Madame Doubtfire."

"That's better."

He leaned down once again, to kiss her. She was already deeply asleep.

"Asleep?" Miranda was astonished. "Are you sure?"

"Quite sure," said Madame Doubtfire. "Fast asleep."

"Extraordinary!" said Miranda.

She looked at the very strange woman trying to sit with elegantly crossed boots at her kitchen table, and thought she ought to check — just in case. It wasn't as if Madame Doubtfire looked like a murderess, or a maniac, or a child molester, or anything like that. It was just that Natalie was not in the habit of letting perfect strangers into the house without a word, or allowing herself to be put to bed by someone she'd never even met before. It was not that Miranda was *worried* exactly, just that Madame Doubtfire was as yet a total stranger, and so very — well — *large*. And Natalie was Miranda's youngest, and so very — well — *small*.

"Would you excuse me for a moment?" asked Miranda. "I'll just pop up for a second. I usually do."

"Do, please," said comforting and comfortable Madame Doubtfire. "I never could settle either, till I was sure mine were tucked in well, and off with the sandman."

Miranda fled upstairs, and Daniel took the opportunity to say a quick hello to Hetty, scratching about contentedly in the freshly spring-cleaned confines of her cage, and to have a good look around the kitchen.

It was, in many ways, exactly as he remembered. The same old floor tiles they'd chosen and laid together — if a bit more scuffed, and with a few lifting corners; the same window blind above the sink — though the flowers in the pattern had faded noticeably; the same gray kitchen cabinets. Miranda, he saw, still kept most of her dry goods in tall glass jars, a habit that used to drive him crazy. He recalled with striking intensity the waves of irritation he used to feel on shopping mornings, faced with the endless clearing up of spills, the time-consuming wiping of sticky fingerprints off clear glass, the insoluble problem of where to put the packet containing the last two ounces of sugar, or flour, or rice, or beans, that never quite fitted inside the jar. Most infuriating of all, he remembered, was being forever unable to judge how much of anything was left. Half a bag of brown sugar is, after all, plainly about half a bag. Two inches of caked sugar coating the sides of a glass jar is a mystery.

But there were changes, too. The walls had been freshly painted in paler blue. The tea towels were different. The back door had a stronger lock. There were far fewer plants now, Daniel noticed, and several of these appeared at death's door.

And Miranda had, he noticed with some irritation, splurged on a new automatic dishwasher. He found it a shade galling that she should have had the nerve to scold him, the until-recently unemployed, for being a few days behind with his payments, when clearly all this time she'd been sufficiently well-heeled herself to stroll out and purchase the most luxurious of kitchen aids. His own apartment could not even boast a washing machine, and Daniel was often to be found down at the Laundromat on the corner, sunk in self-pity, watching the dye seep from his swirling socks, and mystified by all the notices pinned on the wall in exotic languages.

He was still in a sulk when she came back. It took some effort to wipe the scowl off his face, and swing round to greet her.

"The little poppet sleeping nicely?"

"Out like a light," Miranda conceded.

She took a sideways look at this most unusual job applicant as she poured out the coffee. The woman was huge, even taller than Miranda herself, and large-boned. Her features were heavy, and scarcely improved by the layer of pancake makeup and streaks of coloring. Miranda could not see her hair, apart from a few dark wisps creeping out from beneath the extraordinary turban. Though her fingernails were beautifully lacquered, her hands were rough and a little knobby. Her feet were enormous. Miranda gauged the boots at size eleven at the very smallest.

You'd think the very sight of the woman would terrify the average child.

And yet . . . and yet . . .

There was something terribly reassuring about her. She sat like a fortress at the table, reeking of lavender water, solid and steady and imperturbable.

"Such an attractive way of storing food," she was saying in her reverberant, soothing manner. "In those tall glass jars. Worth all the extra trouble, I always think."

"My husband didn't," Miranda recalled. "He hated those jars with a passion. Called them a stupid, fiddly waste of time."

"Kept spilling, did he? Making his little messes all over the table? Not sure how many beans he could tip in? Not knowing where to store the leftovers?"

Miranda smiled, and felt herself relax. It had been a long day at the Lighting Emporium, and she had been more than a little taken aback to bump into this giantess sailing down her own stairs. But Madame

Doubtfire seemed such a nice and understanding lady. And Natalie had slipped off like a sleepy angel, with none of the customary bedtime battles about not wanting to brush her teeth because of the wobbly ones, no pleas for another story, no stalling, no fuss. If only every evening could be as easy. But Natalie was only one of the three. What would the others make of Madame Doubtfire?

"Separated, are you, dear? You and your husband?"

"Divorced."

"Oh, I'm sorry. Marriage can be a great blessing."

"Divorce can be even more of one," answered Miranda.

Madame Doubtfire looked shocked. In order to defend herself, Miranda added:

"My husband was a very difficult man."

"Beat you, did he?" suggested Madame Doubtfire. "Knocked you about a bit, never gave you enough money to put food on the table, frightened the little ones, that kind of thing?"

"Oh, no," said Miranda. "Nothing like that. He's not a violent man, far from it. The children adore him. And insofar as he ever earns any money at all, which isn't very often, he isn't mean."

There was a silence. Then Madame Doubtfire said:

"If you don't mind my saying so, dear, your ex-husband sounds like quite a bit of a catch."

Miranda laughed shortly.

"That's right," she agreed. "A real catch. Like the measles."

At this, Madame Doubtfire began to gather the folds of her salmon pink coat more closely around her.

"Well, dear," she said regretfully. "It's getting on, and I must really think of —"

On an impulse, Miranda reached out and laid a hand on the bulky sleeve, in order to prevent her from rising.

"Oh, please don't go. Please stay and meet the other two children. And then, if you like them . . ."

Madame Doubtfire was staring at the hand on her arm as if it came from outer space. Miranda was about to withdraw when the great bear fingers came down on hers, and patted them gently.

"You'd like me to consider the job?"

"I would. I really would. You seem quite perfect."

Their eyes met for the briefest moment. Miranda looked away, disturbed. To her relief, from outside the back door came sounds of laughter, and a rustling and scuffling, and shadows leaned against the frosted glass. She seized the opportunity to rise from the table and make for the fridge.

"Here they are, back from swimming. And they'll be hungry."

As the door opened, Madame Doubtfire tucked

both legs away primly under the table, and swiveled around to greet the newcomers.

Lydia came in first. Madame Doubtfire reached up nervously and patted her turban.

"Hello, dear. I'm Madame Doubtfire. I've come to keep the house for your mother. I hope we'll be friends."

Staring, Lydia moved aside to make way for her brother, who stared in turn while Madame Doubtfire repeated her brief announcement, and Miranda delved, ill at ease, in the fridge.

There was a silence. Then, suddenly, Christopher scowled horribly and flung his bathing things in a wet lump on the floor.

"Oh, *no! Mother!* It's not *fair!*"

Miranda's back stiffened. In his temper, Christopher kicked the ball of damp things across the kitchen. It fell in a sodden heap behind her heels.

"Why do we have to have a housekeeper anyway, Mother? The house is all right, and so are we! And if you need us to be looked after, why can't Dad do it?"

"Your father?" she shouted. "Don't bring that up again about your father looking after you! Your father is —"

That was as far as she managed to get. For the majestically turbaned Madame Doubtfire had risen to her feet, and raised an imposingly large hand for silence. Turning to Christopher, she asked him gravely,

"Young man, is that the way that you usually speak to your mother?"

Christopher flushed scarlet. Lydia's mouth dropped open. Miranda was so startled she almost dropped the eggs in her hand.

Madame Doubtfire continued sorrowfully:

"It isn't what I would have expected at all. Here's your poor mother, strained from a long, hard day's work earning the wherewithal to pay for that swimming session you've just enjoyed, and tiring herself even more preparing your supper. And just because she's made a responsible arrangement to keep this lovely, lovely home in good order, and you and your sisters well fed and cared for in the early evenings, you lose your temper with her in front of a perfect stranger."

The turban wobbled dangerously as the head was shaken sadly.

"Oh, no. Not what I would have expected at all. How old are you, my dear?"

Unwillingly, and barely audibly, Christopher told her.

Madame Doubtfire's painted eyebrows shot up in horror.

"Mercy!" she gasped. "Quite old enough to know better, I'm sure!"

Christopher scuffed one shoe against the other. He was determined not to surrender.

"But it *isn't* fair," he persisted. "I didn't mean to

be rude, and I'm sorry if I was. But I still don't see why Lydia and Natty and I can't spend the extra time with Dad."

"I'm sure your mother has her reasons . . ."

"Yes," said Miranda with feeling. "I certainly do. I'll tell you what they are, too, if you want." She raised her hand, ready to tick reasons off, one by one, on her beautifully manicured fingers. "For one thing, would you believe it, *their father* —"

Madame Doubtfire coughed sharply.

"Forgive me, dear. But surely you're in the habit of encouraging the children to step out of the room before you indulge in abusing their father?"

Miranda laughed out loud, and not very nicely.

"If I did that, I'd never see them!"

"I see."

The voice was strained, and slightly clipped.

It suddenly occurred to Miranda that, through her outspokenness, she might rashly be spoiling her one and only chance to employ this perfect, if slightly old-fashioned, treasure.

Hastily, she beat an apologetic retreat.

"You're absolutely right, and I'm terribly sorry. I should never have brought their father into this conversation."

"You didn't." Christopher was surly. "You tried to keep him right out, as usual." He turned to his sister for support. "Didn't she, Lydia?"

But Lydia didn't reply. She was staring at Madame Doubtfire with a strange, almost elated, look on her face. Her eyes shone and her feet broke out in little scuffle steps on the floor tiles, as if she were on the verge of dancing.

Madame Doubtfire puckered her glossy brown eyebrows into a warning frown.

"Oooh!"

Lydia seemed to be close to exploding. Nervously, Madame Doubtfire reached for her crocodile handbag and gathered her bulky outdoor garment around her, as if once more compelled to think of leaving. But just at that moment all Lydia's inexplicably pent-up excitement burst through the floodgate of her self-control, decanting forcefully on to her brother.

"Christopher, you're so *stupid!*"

She seized the sleeve of his jacket and pulled him toward her. "Stop being so *difficult,* for heaven's sake!" She tugged at him desperately. "Come on! Upstairs! Now! We've tons of homework and we must get started!" Pushing and heaving with all her strength, she propelled her recalcitrant brother across the room, and shoveled him vigorously through the doorway.

"*So* nice to meet you," she called back to Madame Doubtfire over her shoulder. "I'm sure we'll get along *beautifully.* I *do* hope you agree to take the job. Christopher will be fine, too, I promise, as soon as he *gets used to the idea.* I'll *speak* to him about it. I *know* he'll be pleased."

And, kicking her brother firmly in the shins to shift him the last few inches out of the kitchen, she swiftly drew the door closed behind them.

Sinking back on her chair, Miranda sighed with open relief. Madame Doubtfire's relief was even greater, if slightly less overt. Surreptitiously, she wiped beads of sweat from her forehead, and seemed a little taken aback to see yellowy smears appear on her fingers.

But Miranda didn't notice. She was too busy stretching herself luxuriously in triumph.

"Well, Madame Doubtfire," she said, delighted. "You passed the final test with flying colors."

Madame Doubtfire reached up and patted her turban primly.

"I'm very pleased, dear. Very pleased indeed." She paused momentarily. "They're a spirited pair." Then she added a little warily: "It's none of my business, of course, and stop me at once if I offend you. But if you don't mind my saying so, that son of yours looks to me to be sorely in need of a firm hand."

Miranda smiled.

"I quite agree," she told Madame Doubtfire. "And the job's *yours*."

5

Finding a Role in Life

A couple of weeks later, Madame Doubtfire was leaning on the banister of the upstairs landing, scratching a hairy leg and smoking a cheroot, when Lydia came out of her bedroom with her arms full of tattered comic books.

"You shouldn't smoke," Lydia scolded, dumping the untidy pile on the floor outside Christopher's bedroom. "You'll get black lungs."

Madame Doubtfire narrowed her eyes, and blew a stream of cheroot smoke sideways into the landing curtains. She peeled the blackened stub from between her lips, and spat out a wayward flake of tobacco.

"Listen, my sugarplum," she said. "When I was

young, back in the good old days before I married your mother, I drank my whisky in peace, and smoked my cigarettes without disturbance. That happy time is far, far in the past. But if occasionally in my exhausting middle years I'm driven to down the odd half pint of beer, or drag on the occasional cigar, I'll thank you to keep off my back."

She took another deep drag from the cheroot.

"Just press on with the tidying, honey-bunch. If these bedrooms aren't super tidy by the time your mother gets home, your humble servant here might get the sack."

Lydia pressed on with the tidying. Christopher carried his overflowing wastepaper basket out in the hall, and sighed to see yet another heap of his possessions deposited there by his sister.

"I don't see why it's always us who has to clean up," he grumbled. "It's you who gets paid."

"It all goes toward your damn child support."

Madame Doubtfire stuck the cheroot stub back in her mouth, and lifted her arms to settle the turban more securely on her head.

"Anyway, I'm not good at keeping a house looking nice, you know that. It's one of the reasons your mother divorced me."

She hitched her skirt up higher, revealing an expanse of beefy thigh, and settled herself on the broad ledge of the windowsill, between the pots of spring-flowering azaleas.

"Gardens, now, they're another matter . . ."

She stared out. The carefully plucked and burnished eyebrows crumpled with concern as she looked down at the miserable ranked rows of Miranda's purple sprouting broccoli and winter drumheads.

"By now I really should have limed that vegetable patch . . ."

While Lydia and Christopher continued to scuttle in and out of their respective bedrooms, returning each other's library books and pens, emptying water glasses down the bathroom sink, and dropping crumpled garments into the two matching wicker laundry baskets, Madame Doubtfire leaned back against the window and stared morosely across into next door's garden.

"That Mrs. Hooper's left the door of her shed wide open again. The rain will get in and rot her tools." She turned in sudden outrage. "Do you know what that wretched woman did while you two were at school today?"

"No," Christopher said, passing with Lydia's radio in his arms. "What did that wretched woman do while we were at school?"

Madame Doubtfire clutched at her turban.

"She *only* ripped out a perfectly splendid japonica — tore it away from the wall in a frenzy of horticultural vandalism. That's all she did!"

"Perhaps she wanted the space for something else," suggested Lydia. "Would you pull your knees back so I can get past with this vacuum cleaner?"

Obligingly, Madame Doubtfire lifted her skirts and drew back two enormous hairy knees.

"Very likely," she said. Her lip curled up so far in scorn that the cheroot nearly scorched it. "Room for some flashy supermarket rose, I have no doubt." She sighed, exhaling clouds of blue smoke. "How that woman has the gall to show her face each week at art class, I shall never know. As far as I can make out from all her scrubby renderings of my fine physique, she has no more aesthetic sense than a toilet brush, no more sensitivity than a flagstone. Eight times she's done me now! Eight times! That's sitting and lying and standing in all sorts of positions. She's done me draped in muslin, and with colored lights flashing all over my body. She's done me in chalk and charcoal and pencil and oils, in watercolors and crayons and pastels and, last week, God help us, even clay. That's eight different ways I've turned out so far: pin-headed, hunchbacked, bandy-legged, wall-eyed, wry-necked, ape-armed, barrel-chested and, as a final blow to my self-esteem when a small lump of her clay fell off last week, apparently unmanned." Madame Doubtfire scowled horribly. "I'm wasted on the woman, truly I am. She is impervious to natural beauty."

"I don't know," Christopher mused in passing. "She seems to like me . . ."

"You fail to qualify on either count," Madame

Doubtfire observed tartly. Inspecting the clogged end of her cheroot, she pushed the window open behind her and flipped ash toward Mrs. Hooper's laburnum.

"My God!" she cried, almost falling out of the window in anguish. "The woman's planting her dahlias now!"

"It *is* her garden," Lydia pointed out. "Why shouldn't she plant her dahlias?"

"In *March*? Are you *mad*?"

Gripping the turban tightly with one hand, and holding the smoldering cheroot safely below the level of the window with the other, Madame Doubtfire leaned out.

"Dearie," she warbled over the lawn. "Must *warn!* Plant them out now, and your sweet dahlias will be *slain* by the frost!"

She drew in her turbaned head, and slammed the window shut again.

"Absurd! Needs telling every single year. I must have warned her half a dozen times when I was your father." She heaved a massive sigh. "I'll tell you the trouble with that Hooper woman: she simply cannot take advice. I suppose that I'll have to go down there and stop her. I needed to talk to her anyway, about her bad leaf curl."

Christopher stopped shaking out the comforter. He hated it when, as he tended to think of it to himself, "his father took Madame Doubtfire into the garden."

He feared the possibility of discovery, with all the terrible consequences when the knowledge was passed, as it would be, to his mother.

"Don't go down in the garden. You'll be ages. We're starving. What about our supper?"

Madame Doubtfire pushed open the bathroom door, and dropped her cheroot stub into the toilet bowl.

"Listen," she said. "I count you in after school. I check your simultaneous equations. I wash your underwear. You can't expect me to do all the shopping and cooking, too."

Christopher was outraged.

"Haven't you even *shopped?*"

Madame Doubtfire drowned her absence of positive response to this question by flushing the toilet.

"Isn't there *anything* to eat?" Christopher persisted.

The cheroot stub spun merry circles in the bowl, which drained and refilled. The stub stayed on the surface, circling gently.

"Nothing at *all?*"

Madame Doubtfire shrugged.

"I suppose there's always quail . . ."

"*Quail?*" Christopher was horrified. "Do you mean *Hetty?*"

Madame Doubtfire inspected her fingertips.

"Hetty is quail . . . ," she said. "Quails are nourishing . . ."

Lydia appeared in her doorway, quite as appalled as her brother.

"Are you two talking about cooking *Hetty?*"

"Why not?" Madame Doubtfire picked delicately at the orchid-pink lacquer embellishing her fingernails. "I noticed a rather nice-looking recipe only a couple of days ago. Quail and artichoke salad." The glossy eyebrows furrowed. "It might be a little difficult, though. One of the ingredients was juniper berries. I don't suppose either of you two is prepared to climb over the fence and nick one or two off Mrs. Hooper's dwarf juniper?"

"No!" Christopher shouted.

"No!" Lydia echoed.

Madame Doubtfire leaned over the banister.

"Natalie!" she trilled. "Up here, dear. Quickly. Madame Doubtfire needs your help."

"Oh, no, you don't!" said Christopher. "Lydia could just make us all a tuna fish salad."

"You could just make it yourself," Lydia retorted with some irritation.

"I *wish* I could remember exactly how this recipe went," Madame Doubtfire brooded. "What *was* it now? *Reserve the legs and carcass for the sauce. Sauté the quail trimmings in hot fat in a pan.* . . . Which bits do you suppose the trimmings are, dears? The little legs . . . ?"

"I'll make the tuna fish salad," Christopher hastily capitulated.

"I'll make some pudding," Lydia compromised.

Entirely content with these arrangements, Madame Doubtfire threw open the window once again, and throbbed down to Mrs. Hooper:

"I'll tell you what's coming up very nicely *indeed* this year, dear —"

Christopher shoveled the last of the mess out of sight under his bed, while Lydia slammed the vacuum cleaner away in the landing cupboard. Satisfied with her observations on the current condition of Mrs. Hooper's brussels sprouts, Madame Doubtfire closed the window, giving no more than a gracious Queen Motherly wave through the glass in response to Mrs. Hooper's abruptly muted anxieties about galloping club root.

"I can't *think* why she's worrying about club root," she confided to Lydia and Christopher, just as Natalie appeared at the top of the stairs in response to the recent call for her assistance. "Club root is the least of Mrs. Hooper's problems. To look at her vegetable plot, you'd think the woman only had three gardening tools: the chainsaw, the pickax, and the flame-thrower."

"That's funny," Natalie told her. "That's what my daddy always used to say."

Daniel stared at his younger daughter. He shook his head, baffled. Each of his children had, he knew, developed a different way of coping with the bizarre situation with which he had, without warning, presented them. Lydia's attitude toward his two, sometimes merging, identities was one of detached and laconic amusement. Christopher's was keenly protective: he was ever prepared and preparing against the dreaded moment of discovery. And both of these ways of coping made sense to Daniel. But Natalie's method of handling her father's double personality was very odd, very odd indeed.

All through the first few days, Daniel recalled, she had been worried — terribly, terribly worried. As he sailed confidently around the house masquerading as Madame Doubtfire, Natalie had stood in anguish, consumed with anxiety, watching him with the deepest unease, and jumping out of her skin each time the front door opened, or the telephone rang. The mere mention of Miranda's name put her into a tizzy. Clearly the whole arrangement disturbed her so much that Daniel began to wonder if it might not have been a disastrous mistake, more likely to upset Natty with his presence than comfort her for his absences.

Then, as it now seemed looking back on it, everything changed.

To Natty, he seemed to become two entirely separate people. Gradually, as the days went by, it was as if Madame Doubtfire became more and more real, and Daniel was being pushed out of her entirely. This seemed to make Natalie more comfortable. Where she had been almost a nervous wreck, once again she became her placid, equable self. She stopped busying herself with crayons and tiny plastic animals anywhere in the house but where he happened to be, avoiding him as much as possible, and took instead to trailing happily around in his wake, chattering with ease, telling him all about her day at school, her quarrels and games in the playground, and her mother's occasional men friends.

"She's going out with Sam tonight," she'd say, adding wistfully: "I wish she wasn't."

"Why, dear?"

"I just wish she were going out with Mr. Lennox."

"Why?" Daniel persisted, suddenly worried beyond measure lest this Sam were cruel, or insensitive, or even just cold to his precious Natty.

"Because Sam always brings boring old flowers. Mr. Lennox brings chocolates, special big boxes with no horrible strawberry creams."

"I quite like strawberry creams myself, dear."

"So does my daddy."

It seemed best to say nothing. But it was, Daniel found, thoroughly disquieting to be leaning over the sink, idly rinsing a dish or two under the tap, and find he was listening to his own daughter telling how, in her father's kitchen, the soap bar was encrusted with nasty bits of grit which scratched the palms of her hands when she washed them, and his washing-up brush was so bald it couldn't clean dishes. He learned the hard way that it was better not to rear up as Daniel on these occasions, defending his honor on such small matters. It made her nervous. Indeed, after a while her clear division of these two protectors in her life became so unyielding that whenever Daniel made the mistake of letting the mask slip, if only for a moment — used his own voice to call her from one room to another, swept her up onto his shoulders, swore at the vacuum cleaner in a Danielish fashion — then Natalie fell silent and lowered her eyes, grew most uncomfortable and drew away, wandered off into another room and stayed there. But so long as Daniel remained foursquare in the heavy brogue shoes he had bought Madame Doubtfire — along with a new pinless turban and several nice blouses — then Natalie stayed happy and at ease in his presence, more than willing to help him with all sorts of little household tasks, eager to confide her secrets, easy to cuddle.

So Daniel tailored Madame Doubtfire's days to avoid any manifestations of Daniel. He learned to drink his lunchtime beer from a porcelain teacup. He formed the habit of smoking his occasional cheroot upstairs on the landing, where he could blow the smoke out of the window, and flush the telltale stub away the moment he heard little Natalie approaching. And, toward teatime each day, when he shaved closely for the second time, he made a point of shutting the bathroom door between himself and his small daughter.

It was all strange, very strange. But nothing stays strange for too long, and soon he found he had become accustomed to hearing old conversations with himself faithfully reported back, as Natalie companionably followed Madame Doubtfire around the house in the afternoons.

"Hand me that coat hanger, would you, dear? I'll just hang this slip of your mother's away in her wardrobe."

Natalie obediently leaned over the edge of the bed she was rolling on, and picked the hanger off the floor.

"It's chewed," she said critically. "Chewed at the edges. Daddy says you should never, *ever* chew plastic."

"He's quite right there, dear. You never know what you're chewing with plastic."

"Yes, that's what Daddy says. He says it's all right to suck it, if you *must,* but biting and chewing are out, right out, and he *means* it."

"Well, he says no more than the truth, dear. And, if I were you, I should pay very close attention to anything your father tells you."

"I do."

"Quite right."

"And I'm going to knit him a tie for his birthday."

"Are you, dear? That will be nice. I expect he'll like that."

"It's going to be pink."

"I'm sure he'll love it."

"It's a surprise."

"Indeed, yes. Pass me that bra, dear, would you? That lacy thing lying over the chair back."

Natalie passed it over, and Madame Doubtfire inspected it critically before dropping it onto the pile for the laundry.

Natalie giggled.

"*Undies worn twice*

"*Are not very nice,*" she sang merrily.

"That's all very well for those who can afford a washing machine," said Madame Doubtfire, somewhat cryptically.

"Daddy can't," mourned Natalie, and then, reminded: "He'll have to try to keep my pink tie clean when he wears it." She sighed. "*If* he wears it . . ."

Madame Doubtfire assured her confidently: "If you knit your father a pink tie for his birthday, he'll wear it, I'm quite sure."

"That's what Lydia says. She says he has whole drawerfuls of horrible ties, and he wears those, so he'll wear mine."

"Lydia said that, did she, dear?"

"Yes. Yes, she did."

Natalie folded her legs beneath her on the bed, and looked thoughtful.

"I tried to phone him."

"Did you, dear? Why?"

"To ask him if he liked pink."

"When, dear?"

"Just now. While you were in the bathroom. But

he was out." She picked absentmindedly at the fringe of the counterpane. "He's out a *lot* now. He always used to be in when I phoned him."

"Natalie —"

"What?"

"It doesn't matter. Never mind."

But it did matter, and he could tell that she did mind. He minded, too — so much so that when Miranda finally returned home very late from work that evening, and dumped a huge box of substandard light fittings down on the kitchen table in a vile mood, he was still far, far too keyed-up to have the sense to postpone his fictitious report of a telephone message.

"Dear, just before I take off — their father called . . ."

Lydia and Christopher, he noticed, only pricked up their ears with amusement and interest; but Natalie looked absolutely delighted.

Miranda screwed her face up into an exhausted grimace.

"Oh, God. Just what I need!"

"Dear?"

"Never mind. When did he call? Don't tell me. Lunchtime."

Madame Doubtfire was puzzled.

"Lunchtime? Why lunchtime, particularly?"

"He just has this incredibly annoying habit of always seeming to call here at mealtimes."

"Oh. Does he, dear?"

Irritated, Daniel made a mental note to call her during breakfast the following morning.

"Yes, he does." She reached out for her cup of tea. "Well, what did he want *this* time?"

"*This* time?" Madame Doubtfire looked little short of reprovingly at her. "You could hardly accuse him of being importunate, dear. They are his children as much as yours, and he's only called a couple of times since I began to work for you."

"Yes," Natalie said sorrowfully. "He never seems to call now."

Miranda had had a very hard day at work. She was in no mood to be sympathetic.

"He shouldn't need to call at all. You see him quite regularly, and he must know the schedule by heart."

"Really, dear!" Madame Doubtfire was thoroughly disapproving now. "I thought it very nice of him to call. Not everything in life fits in a schedule. The children can phone him whenever they want. Why shouldn't he phone them? If fathers and children need contact with one another, it's not the mother's place to interfere."

Miranda shrugged off the lecture.

"What did he *want?*"

Under the stress of this near altercation, the answer Madame Doubtfire came out with was rather more lavish than anything previously planned.

"He wants to take them to the theater on Saturday afternoon."

Natalie squealed with pleasure. Miranda scowled.

"This Saturday? But it's *my* weekend this week!"

"But you're away until six on Saturday, dear. You told me so yourself, when you asked me to come in specially. You have to go to a Home Lighting Conference in Wolverhampton. You said so."

"It's still my weekend," sulked Miranda.

Madame Doubtfire gathered herself up.

"Pardon me for saying so, dear. But isn't your attitude getting to be a hint dog-in-the-mangerish?"

Miranda's scowl deepened.

"Oh, honestly! What a great nuisance!"

Christopher rushed forward.

"Oh, *please*, Mother. Let us go with Dad on Saturday. I haven't been to the theater for years!"

"I can't *remember* the last time I went to a play," said Lydia.

"I've never been to one at all," said Natalie.

"Yes, you have," Madame Doubtfire corrected her firmly. Then she hastily corrected herself. "I'm sure you must have, dear. Quite sure. I expect that you've simply forgotten."

"We've all forgotten," Christopher said. "It's been so long. Please let us go, Mother. Please, please, *please*."

"Oh, I don't know!" Miranda glowered. "It's very bad of your father to try to upset the schedule like this. How do I know he'll bring you back in good time? You know what he's like. And he probably hasn't even got the tickets yet, anyway. That would be absolutely typical of him. You three will get all excited, and then he'll turn up here on Saturday and tell you that all the seats were sold out. I'll come home worn out from Wolverhampton, and have to think of something to cheer you all up. It's happened that way often enough before! Oh, what a *nuisance* that man can be!"

"But Mother! If he gets tickets, can we go?"

"Oh, honestly! How *annoying!*" said Miranda in a decided manner, as if the whole matter was settled, and to her total dissatisfaction, at that.

Genuinely at a loss, Christopher asked the air around him:

"Does Mother mean we can go?"

Miranda's expression was black with irritation. She gnawed her fingers. "Oh, I don't know! What a bother! How *dare* he? This is *typical!*"

It was clearly for Madame Doubtfire to step in, and step in she did.

"I think this is your mother's quaint way of saying you may, dears," she told them. "And you're very fortunate, too, in my opinion. It must be a privilege to go to the theater with Daniel Hilliard. He's a very fine actor, very fine indeed."

Annoyed beyond measure with Miranda, she sailed closer and closer to the wind. "Indeed, I once saw him on a stage myself . . ."

"Really?" Lydia and Christopher were grinning, but Natalie was thrilled. "What was he? What part did he play?"

Suddenly, Madame Doubtfire looked stricken. In Christopher's mind there surfaced the faintest, far-away memory of going to see his very first pantomime ever. A tall man dressed in woman's clothing cavorted on the brightly lit stage. His mother had leaned over, and whispered in his ear: "See! There's your father, the one doing that dance with the musical sausages. He's Madame Doubtfire."

"Your bus!" cried Christopher. "You mustn't miss your bus!"

One cue was all it took. Gratefully, Madame Doubtfire lunged under the table for her handbag, and swept up her coat.

"Bye, dears," she warbled. "Until tomorrow!"

And blowing them kisses over her shoulder, she fled.

Miranda shook her head. It was hard to fault Madame Doubtfire. Indeed, Miranda had popped up-stairs for just a moment to wash her hands after carrying that dusty box of broken light fittings, and the house was a pleasure to look at, truly it was. All those things she'd left scattered around her bedroom after her evening with Sam had been discreetly tidied away, and Lydia and Christopher's bedrooms could not have looked nicer. But, nonetheless, sometimes it seemed to Miranda that she had hired the strangest house-keeper on the earth.

She turned to her son who was looking, she thought, just a tiny bit rattled.

"Christopher," she said. "How are you finding Madame Doubtfire?"

Nerve-racking, Christopher thought privately, recalling with some bitterness the soggy cheroot stub he had fished out of the toilet bowl only moments before his mother's arrival.

"Fine," he assured her. "Absolutely fine."

Miranda fiddled with her teaspoon.

"She's very, well, *strange*, don't you think?"

"No," Christopher said firmly. "I don't find her strange. Neither does Lydia. Nor does Natalie."

"But she's so very, well, *large,* for one thing."

"She's not *that* large," Christopher argued. "She's only a tiny bit taller than you."

"But I'm terribly tall. I'm only a little bit shorter than your father. And Madame Doubtfire is even taller than I am."

"So?"

He sounded sufficiently defensive to startle his mother. She wondered suddenly if this were the first sign of some as yet unnoticed strain of chivalry in her son.

"Well, she is *big,* you must admit."

"No." Christopher was obdurate. "I don't think she's big."

"Oh, really, Christopher!"

Exasperated, Miranda turned to her elder daughter.

"What do you think of her, Lydia?"

"Well . . ." Lydia grinned. "She is a *little* strange."

Miranda was relieved. One of her children, at least, still had some sense.

"*Isn't* she? She really is strange. But don't you think it's worked out well? Better than it would if you spent extra time with your father?"

There was a pause before Lydia answered.

"I wouldn't say *better*. But, then again, I wouldn't say *worse,* either. I think I'd have to say — *different*."

Satisfied with this, Miranda turned to Natalie.

"And what do you think, Natty? Do you like Madame Doubtfire?"

"Oh, yes!" Natalie's testimony was immediate. "I like her a *lot*." Since her brother and sister were smirking at her, she added rashly: "I think that probably Madame Doubtfire is my most favorite person."

Mischievously, Lydia asked:

"But what about Daddy?"

Natalie stared, paralyzed with horror, at her sister. She looked, Miranda thought, positively anguished. She drew breath, let it out, then, desperate, drew breath again.

"I th-think —" she stuttered. "I think — I think —" And then, as the solution mercifully struck her, she finished in a tone of triumph:

"I think I like them both *exactly the same!*"

6

Happy Families

Hearing Miranda's heels tapping up the garden path the next evening, Madame Doubtfire paused in her watering.

"Here comes your mother, home from running the Empire."

Miranda caught the last few words as she stepped through the front door.

"Running the *Empire?*" she queried from the hall.

"Sorry, dear," called Madame Doubtfire. "I meant the Emporium. I often mix up those two words."

Christopher looked nervously at Lydia as she snickered, keeping her head well down over her homework. When Miranda came in the room, she didn't notice her daughter's amusement. As usual, she was exhausted and her feet ached. Glancing appreciatively toward the coal fire burning in the grate, she flung herself down in the nearest armchair, and pried off her uncomfortable shoes.

"The cup that cheers, dear?"

Gratefully, Miranda reached out and took it. The tea, like the warm fire and Madame Doubtfire herself, was perfect. All her doubts of the evening before forgotten, Miranda blessed the day she took this huge, ungainly pantomime dame into her family. Maybe Madame Doubtfire was a queer coot. But Miranda was first and foremost a businesswoman, and she had learned to judge by results. The results of this particular decision were little short of magical, she decided. The children were steadier and happier, the house ran like clockwork, and the woman made meatloaf as good as Daniel's. At times like these, stretched in an armchair in front of a ready, blazing fire, tea in hand, with the elder two already settled at the table immersed in their homework and Natalie peaceably shunting little plastic creatures around her feet, Miranda could not think how the four of them had ever managed before Madame Doubtfire's arrival.

Daily, the woman continued to astonish. No doubt at this very moment a nourishing supper was simmering in the oven, yesterday's ironing pile had been dispersed to drawers and wardrobes around the house, the quail had been fed and watered, and the kitchen was spotless. But still Madame Doubtfire was on her feet, turban nodding, fretting about the plants on the bookshelf.

"This tradescantia isn't doing at all well," she was saying. "I *thought* it was too far gone when I came."

"It looks all right to me," said Lydia. "Sort of lean and wiry and interesting."

Madame Doubtfire regarded her with barely disguised ill favor.

"Tradescantias come from the jungle," she informed her. "They are supposed to be lush. Whereas the number of leaves on this one could be counted on the fingers of one slightly abnormal hand."

"But you've worked wonders with the rest of the plants," Miranda consoled her treasure. "They've absolutely flourished since you took over."

Indeed they had. Botanical salvation was assured. Even some of the most sickly cases had revived. "I don't like the look of that black-eyed Susan," Madame Doubtfire had muttered on the first day, as she struggled to tie the bow on her brand-new apron. "And that weeping fig is little more than good kindling." She'd set to work with plant food and mist sprays, leaf wipes and slim green support sticks. And now the pinks were all pinker, the climbers climbed higher, leaves flourished, buds burgeoned, and the tendrils of the plants in the hanging baskets had grown so long and thick and curly they tangled in Miranda's hair as she stepped in the porch every evening.

Madame Doubtfire was complacent.

"No, I don't think I've done your plants much harm . . ."

"Harm!" Miranda feigned outrage. "Why, you've performed little miracles all over the house. You're like my ex-husband. He has green fingers."

Behind her, she heard a little snort, and wondered if Lydia was coming down with a spring cold. But before she could look around and inspect her for signs of incipient sickness, Madame Doubtfire leaned forward, tapping her wrist to reclaim her attention.

"Shocking state they were in when I arrived, dear. Simply shocking! I barely managed to save the African violets. A couple more months, and your busy Lizzies would have gone, too. I have to say it: you'd been very neglectful."

"I did try," Miranda sighed. "It's just that I'm no good with plants. I tried so hard to take care of them, but, after Daniel left, they just became more and more miserable."

"Poor plants," Natalie sympathized softly at her feet.

Miranda rattled on.

"Last spring, seeing the way the pinks were going, I even tried to take a few cuttings. I stuffed them in a jar of water, and shoved them out of the way on that box beside the boiler down in the basement."

"No point in letting your plants get uppity," observed Madame Doubtfire in what struck Miranda as an uncharacteristically sardonic manner.

"They did all right," she defended herself. "After a few weeks I even noticed that out of the bottom they'd started to sprout those little white things."

"Roots," said Madame Doubtfire. "Those little white things at the bottom are called roots."

"So then I bunged them in a few rusty paint pots I'd filled with that thick brown stuff — what's it called?"

"Soil," Madame Doubtfire said. "We of a horticultural bent call it soil."

"No!" Miranda remembered. "It was Mrs. Nimble Green Thumbs Number Two Compost!"

She sat back happily.

"Yes?" inquired Madame Doubtfire, after it became apparent that Miranda considered her tale fully told. "And what happened then?"

"Oh. Then they died."

Madame Doubtfire did make the effort to look just a tiny bit astonished. But she couldn't resist a botanical postmortem.

"You probably starved them. Or parched them. Or drowned them."

"Or blighted them," suggested Lydia.

"Or left them in a draft," said Christopher, pushing his nervousness to one side in the effort not to be outdone in all these flourishes of horticultural expertise.

"I bet they were really unhappy," said Natalie. "Pinks simply *hate* to get their feet wet."

"They do resent wet compost, yes," Madame Doubtfire agreed.

Miranda stared. She hadn't realized Natalie knew anything about plants. But more and more frequently now, her younger daughter was astonishing her, coming out with outlandish snippets of information she was unlikely to have picked up at school. Clearly, when she reached home each afternoon, she trailed around the house behind Madame Doubtfire as she watered and misted and fertilized and pruned, and they chatted, exchanging botanical confidences. Miranda was pleased. All too frequently in the last few years, she had been forced to regard herself as an unresponsive and distant parent, too often absent earning their living, too often frazzled by the day's events at the Emporium, too often simply too damn tired, to sit and listen with any pleasure to her children's conversation. It was a great and growing relief to Miranda that Madame Doubtfire had turned out to be such a great marvel. Everything was easier, and, as a result, everything was somehow becoming more pleasant. Even the hours spent at work were less of a strain, since, for the first time since she could remember, Miranda was able to stop worrying entirely about whether she might return home to confusion or upset.

The woman was totally capable. Even more admirable, she was totally decisive. There wasn't a shred of "wait-and-see" about her. And unlike every other link in the seemingly endless chain of women and girls Miranda had employed over the years to tide her over working hours, Madame Doubtfire had never once, to Miranda's knowledge, fallen back on the tired old baby-sitting formula: "I'm not sure about that. You'd better wait and ask your mother."

Quite the reverse. She actually seemed immune to the notion that the children belonged, first and foremost, to Miranda. She seemed sincerely to believe she held invested within her all the authority of a real parent. Even now, with Miranda right there sipping her second cup of tea and stretching her toes toward the fire's warmth, Madame Doubtfire suddenly told Christopher quite sharply to drop his chair back on four legs, and suggested to little Natalie that she might please everyone in the room if she were to refrain from exploring up her nose with her finger.

At first, Miranda had found this easy assumption of equally shared authority a little disconcerting. But she relaxed into it with simple relief once the benefits of the arrangement became evident, once she realized how oiled and easy it made whole areas of daily life which had for so long now been tiresome and scratchy.

"I've warned Lydia there'll be no trip to the theater with her father tomorrow unless she's made some real progress with that history project," Madame Doubtfire was saying. even now. "Isn't it a pity you weren't back sooner! I made Christopher polish all the shoes, and those look as though they could do with a brush-up."

She rose, and shook out her heavy tweed skirt.

"I'll miss another bus at this rate. Shall I just bank up the fire for you before I go?"

Lifting the scuttle with one enormous hand, she swung it back as if it were as light as air, and shot a shower of coal into the grate.

"By the way, I have arranged with Natalie that, from now on, it's her job to unload the dishwasher."

"You are a treasure, Madame Doubtfire," Miranda murmured. "Better by far than a husband."

"Surely that would depend on whose, dear?"

Miranda giggled.

"Well, better than mine, for a start."

"Oh, yes?" Madame Doubtfire hesitated in the action of reaching for her crocodile handbag.

Behind their mother's chair, Lydia and Christopher caught one another's eye. Christopher bit his lip. He always became anxious when his father postponed his departure for too many minutes after Miranda's arrival. To Christopher's way of thinking, once Miranda was in the house, each word, each gesture from Madame Doubtfire was a risk. Hazards lay everywhere. At any moment some terrible accident might occur. Madame Doubtfire might drop something heavy on her foot, and let rip with one of Daniel's unmistakable curses. Her turban might roll off her head. She might forget to bolt the bathroom door, and, surprised in privacy, surprise in turn. Even now, who was to say that in the room's stealing, seductive warmth, Madame Doubtfire might not, without thinking, roll up the sleeves of her frilled blouse, exposing two muscle-bound, hairy forearms?

But Lydia was grinning with amusement. She quite enjoyed these moments when her father, precariously concealed in this, his daily masquerade, enticed Miranda into gems of disclosure and reminiscence about the bad old married days. It was dangerous, yes; but it was fascinating, too, to listen to Madame Doubtfire winkling out of Miranda indiscretions that gave Lydia her first glimpse of insight into the reasons why the marriage had failed. She had, over the last few weeks, been disabused of more than one mistaken notion about one or other of her parents. More than one little gap in her knowledge had been filled. It was worth tiptoeing through this minefield to hear intriguing little details about the past.

And she wasn't alone. Daniel, too, seemed prepared to risk discovery — indeed, seemed almost as though he were even getting to enjoy the brief daily flirtation with danger, the perilous games of verbal blind man's buff, with his former wife trapped forever in the role of the blind man.

"He was no treasure, then, your ex-husband?"

"God, no!" Miranda reached up to pull the pins out of her glorious hair. "I'll tell you what was wrong with him."

"Yes. Do, dear."

Christopher squirmed uneasily over his home-work. Lydia pricked up her ears. Natalie, too, looked up from her plastic menagerie.

"My husband was —" Miranda took the deepest breath as the sheer enormity of what Daniel was struck her again, in all its fullness and richness, after the years of partial release. "— *the most irresponsible man that I have ever had the misfortune to meet, let alone marry.*"

"Oh, surely not!"

"Oh, yes! He is so irresponsible, he shouldn't have been trusted with a log in a field, let alone with a wife and a house and some children."

"What did he *do,* dear?"

"I'll tell you what he did." Angry at the mere memory, Miranda tossed her head. The dazzling red hair tumbled down. She shook it fiercely and it fanned out around her face, making her look like an avenging angel.

"*Fiery, mud-slinging baggage!*" thought Daniel. "*Pathological exaggerator. Judas! False witness!*"

"Yes, dear?" he prompted sweetly.

"Listen," said Miranda.

Everyone listened.

"The first time I knew that I'd married a mad-man," began Miranda, "was my wedding day. I was nineteen. I wore a long, white gown and orange flow-ers in my hair. It was a glorious spring afternoon, with fluffy mountains of cloud moving across the bluest sky. Everyone we invited had come, except for two miserable uncles I never really wanted anyway. It might have been a perfect day . . ."

"I've heard about this, I think," said Christopher, doing his utmost to check her in the hope that his father would pick up his handbag and go home.

"Shh!" Natalie scolded. "We're listening to the story!"

"The Registry Office was in the Town Hall. When I arrived, your father was already standing on the steps, watching a woman in the entrance to the supermarket next door."

"I *know* I've heard this one," said Christopher, still hoping to forestall her.

"Be *quiet!*" Natalie hushed him fiercely.

"The woman was trying to give away kittens. Beside her was a cardboard box, and sweet little kitten ears and pink noses kept peeping over the top, and falling back. She had a homemade sign saying the kittens needed homes desperately, and any that hadn't been adopted by the time the supermarket closed that night would have to be taken to the pound."

Natalie was sitting spellbound. Her mother went on:

"I knew why Daniel was taking such an interest. His own cat had given birth to an enormous litter of kittens only eight weeks before, and he still hadn't managed to find homes for any of them, even though we were about to go off on our honeymoon."

"Where?" Lydia asked.

"The north of Scotland," Madame Doubtfire told her.

Miranda was astonished.

"How do you know that?"

There was a slightly uncomfortable pause before Madame Doubtfire explained.

"You remember those framed photographs stuffed away out of sight at the back of your wardrobe, dear? I tidied them last week, and couldn't help noticing one showed a fine looking figure of a man stealing a kiss from you over a beach café table."

"But how did you guess that was my honeymoon?"

"Well!" Madame Doubtfire looked a little startled. "Kissing in *public,* dear?"

"And how did you guess it was Scotland?"

"Recognized the cliffs, dear. And then the weather looked so very unpleasant . . ."

"Please!" Natalie begged. "What about the poor kittens? Please tell about the kittens. *Please!*"

Distracted, Miranda took up the story as Christopher breathed again and Madame Doubtfire unobtrusively wiped sweat from her palms.

"As soon as he saw me, your father bounded

down the steps. 'Listen,' he said. 'I've just been talking to that woman. She had six kittens when she started. Apparently she stood there all day yesterday in the pouring rain, and all this morning through those nasty hail showers, and all this afternoon. Now she has only two kittens left, and a girl in the shop has promised to take one of those.' "

It was clear from the expression on Natalie's face that this was a great load off her mind.

Miranda carried on.

"We were already late. I took his arm and we walked into the Town Hall. Everyone was waiting, and we were married straight away. Your father was in such a state, he dropped the ring twice."

"You shouldn't need a weatherman to tell you which way the wind is blowing," Madame Doubtfire scolded her gently. "You should have known to back out then, before it was all far, far too late."

"So should he!" Miranda responded tartly.

"Oh, yes, dear. So should he. No doubt about that!"

It struck Lydia suddenly that, if either her father or her mother had backed out at that moment, she and her brother and sister would never have been born. It was the most disturbing notion. As she forced it to the back of her mind, planning to give it some more thought later, Miranda was saying:

"Anyhow, it would never have occurred to me

to back out. I was so happy. I loved him, and I wanted him, and there we were, married at last. We stepped away from the Registrar's desk, and all our friends surged forward to hug us and kiss us and —"

She stopped short.

"And —?"

"And —?"

"And —?"

Daniel forbore from joining the chorus. He knew, only too well, what was coming.

"And your father was gone!"

"Gone?"

"Gone?"

"Gone?"

"Gone! Disappeared. Nowhere to be seen. Slipped away. Vanished."

"What did you *do?*"

"There wasn't much I could do, was there? After a while I sent my brother along to the restroom to see if he was in there. My brother came out shaking his head. So everyone just milled around in the foyer, burning with curiosity, huddled in little groups and whispering, wondering if the bridegroom had had the nerve to cut out after less than one full minute of marriage. My mother was in tears. My father looked murderous."

"Ooh!" breathed Natalie. She tried to imagine her plump and amiable grandfather as a murdering man, and couldn't do it.

"And you?" Lydia was fascinated. "What about you?"

"Me?" Miranda picked at a loose thread in her dress. "I felt as if the skies had tumbled. I was embarrassed, miserable, humiliated and confused. My wedding had become a mockery. For all I knew, everything else was ruined as well."

"It must have been *terrible* for you," said Lydia. She eyed Madame Doubtfire thoughtfully as she spoke.

Madame Doubtfire scowled, and taking this dark look for one of sympathy, Miranda carried on.

"I forced myself to pretend that nothing had happened. I sailed from guest to guest, laughing and chatting and tossing my hair. Whenever anyone slyly asked what had become of Daniel, I insisted he was bound to be back any moment, and was probably planning some wonderful surprise."

"And was he?"

Lydia kept her cool, inscrutable eyes on Madame Doubtfire.

"Well . . ." Miranda answered drily, "it was a surprise . . ."

"What *was* it?"

"Be *patient*. After about twenty minutes, when I was ready to *die* of embarrassment, the usher sidled up to my father and told him we would have to leave. There were other weddings, and we were clogging the foyer. So we all drifted out through the front door, on to the steps. And there was your father."

"Where?"

"At the bottom of the steps, right in front of us. Just leaping off a bus. And in his arms there was a cardboard box."

"The surprise!" shouted Natalie, glad that her father's honor was going to be restored at last.

Miranda glanced at her pityingly, before saying: "Then, in front of *everyone,* with everyone *staring,* your father tucked the box under his arm, rushed up and grabbed me by the wrist. 'Quick!' he hissed. 'She'll be gone any minute!' He practically *shoveled* me down those steps. He bruised my arm. He tore my dress. In full view of everyone, he dragged me over to that poor woman who was still standing, forlorn and exhausted, outside the supermarket, desperate to find a home for her very last kitten. 'Here!' he said to her. 'These are for you!' And do you know what he did?"

Natalie writhed with impatience, desperate to be told.

"He lifted the flap of his cardboard box, and tipped a swirling, furry flurry into her box. The entire litter! Eight more sweet, adorable, vulnerable little kittens! The woman was appalled. Simply appalled! I thought that she was going to faint from the shock. She was so horrified she couldn't speak. And before I could say or do anything, Daniel had hauled me away, dragging me across the busy pavement and thrusting me up on the deck of some passing bus. I struggled to leap off and get back to the woman, but Daniel stopped me. He pinned me up against the No

Spitting sign, and kissed me till the traffic lights had gone green, and the bus was moving too fast for me to risk it."

All the children were staring now, and Madame Doubtfire looked most uncomfortable.

"Then everyone on the bus started clapping. They were applauding Daniel for kissing his brand-new bride with such passion. I was so angry I slapped his face. Everyone frowned, and turned to face the front, whispering between themselves about my bad temper, and how that nice young man had obviously just come from making the worst mistake of his life."

She heaved the most enormous sigh.

"Well, maybe there is something wrong with me. Maybe I look at things in the wrong way. All I can tell you is, I stood on the deck of that bus in my grubby and bedraggled wedding dress, traveling at a steady twenty-five miles an hour away from my own wedding party, and I cried my poor eyes out. I realized that I had just made the terrible, terrible mistake of marrying the most irresponsible man in the world."

There was a long silence. Natalie was thinking about the poor woman with aching legs, forced to stand by the chilly brick wall of the supermarket for two more whole days, or even longer, getting rid of another boxful of kittens. Like an endless school break-time, Natalie thought, with no friends to talk to you, and no good games to keep you warm . . .

Christopher was intrigued that he'd never before

been told this particular story. You'd think, even if his mother wanted to forget it, and his father was ashamed, his grandparents might have brought it up at least once or twice over the years. After all, they must have forked out quite a bit of money for the wedding and the ruined reception party. They must have been upset and angry. Strange that they never mentioned it, even . . .

Lydia wondered whether a traditional wedding inside a proper church might have made any difference — curbed her father's wild behavior, as it were. In the end, she decided it probably wouldn't. The issue was, she thought, one of lack of respect; but not for the wedding ceremony itself, more a lack of respect for her mother's feelings and wishes. Look at the story in one way, and it was funny. Lydia could see that. But looked at only from outside, or down the years. When it happened, it couldn't have seemed either funny or forgivable. And particularly not that kiss on the bus. That was their first married kiss, and he had made of it a sham and a farce. If she'd been in her mother's shoes . . .

"If I'd been you, Mother, I'd have *killed* him!"

The depth of feeling in her daughter's voice astonished Miranda. And Daniel, too. Perturbed, he made an effort to defend himself, pour oil over troubled water.

"All a terribly long time ago, dear. Water under

bridges, and well away. I'm quite sure he got better after you were married."

"On the contrary," said Miranda. "If anything, he got worse."

"How?" Lydia asked.

"Well," said Miranda. "On our honeymoon, he whispered to a rabbi sharing our train compartment all the way from London up to Inverness that every morsel of British Rail food was cooked in pork fat. The poor man would have starved to death if I'd not caught on when we reached York!"

"I've definitely heard that one before," said Christopher. And throwing his former policy of protecting his father to the winds, he added provocatively: "*And* the one about Mrs. Hooper's tomcat getting stuck up the elm tree."

"I don't remember that one," said Lydia.

Madame Doubtfire tried coughing, but nobody heard. They were all listening to Christopher.

"Kittykins got stuck up the elm tree one morning. He was stuck up there all day. When it got so dark he couldn't even see the tidbits spread on the tree roots to tempt him down, Mrs. Hooper panicked. She started borrowing ladders and clattering them about. She kept the whole street awake for hours, calling to the cat and banging garden shed doors and crashing ladders into branches. At two in the morning, Dad lost his temper. He flung the window open, leaned out in his pajamas and yelled: 'Stop all that racket and go to bed!' Mrs. Hooper called back: 'But what about poor Kittykins?' And Dad bellowed at her at the top of his voice: 'For God's sake, woman! You're forty-nine years old! How many cats' skeletons have you *seen* up in trees?' "

"I didn't know that one," said Lydia over Madame Doubtfire's persistent throat-clearing. "I only knew the one where everyone was standing weeping at Uncle Jack's funeral." She smiled at Madame Doubtfire strangely. "And Dad pretended the hearse drove over his foot."

"What happened?" Christopher asked.

"The hearse driver nearly had a heart attack. Dad jumped about on one leg, clutching the other, until he lost his balance suddenly and fell into a freshly dug grave."

"I didn't realize you'd been told that one," said Miranda.

"I heard it from Aunt Ruth," said Lydia. "She told me one day when Dad did something even worse."

"Even worse?" Christopher's ears were practically flapping. "What? Tell us quick!"

Madame Doubtfire's face darkened as Lydia told them.

"It happened a few years ago." There was an unfamiliar shade of menace in her voice that Daniel didn't care for at all. "Aunt Ruth had come to see the baby."

"What baby?" Natalie demanded.

"You," Lydia told her. "You were the baby, Natty. You were so young you couldn't even sit up alone. You could roll over, though, and you rolled over quite a lot."

Natalie giggled, not really believing her sister.

"You were asleep. Aunt Ruth had just changed your diaper on the sofa, and you had fallen asleep right there, between the cushions. She didn't want to risk waking you by picking you up and putting you safely in your crib, but she needed to go to the bathroom. She was desperate, she said. She hadn't had a moment since she arrived. Dad just happened to come in the room, so Aunt Ruth asked him to watch you. 'Don't let the baby roll off the sofa,' she warned, and then she hurried out of the room. She shut the bathroom door and slid the bolt across. She'd just taken down her pants and sat on the seat when she heard the most awful *thud* from the living room. She said: 'Just like a baby falling on its head on the floor!' She flew out of the toilet with her pants all tangled around her ankles."

Lydia paused. Madame Doubtfire reached under the chair for her handbag.

"It was Dad, of course. He had deliberately stamped on the floor."

Madame Doubtfire rose, clutching her handbag to her bosom. Her face was set, her voice chilly.

"I think I'd best be off now," she informed them.

"I'm sure these little stories about the children's father will keep you all amused till bedtime." A thin rill of sarcasm rippled beneath the frost in her voice. "I must say, dear, I'd simply no idea how *terribly* you must have suffered."

Miranda failed to discern the jibe.

"It was *awful*," she agreed. "Such a great *strain*. I am a little straitlaced by nature, I'd be the first to admit it. But sometimes it seems to me that Daniel can act any part in the world to perfection except that of a normal, responsible human being!" She sighed. "Maybe that's what attracted me in the first place. I'm so very serious and careful myself, maybe I thought he made a nice change, maybe I even thought he would change me." She sighed again, even more heavily. "But marriage doesn't seem to work that way. People don't change, except a little around the edges. And so I was miserable. Living with Daniel was like living on a knife edge. I never knew what he might do next." She spread her hands in almost the same way Daniel did when he was speaking about her. "In the end, you know, it wasn't even the irresponsibility I minded the most. It was the embarrassment. The sheer, hideous, nerve-racking *embarrassment* of the outrageous things he did."

Behind her mother's chair, Lydia ostentatiously wrenched open a French book and stuck her fingers in her ears. She was suddenly very angry indeed with her father, and wanted him to know it. It seemed to

Lydia deeply wrong and offensive that her mother should be opening her heart so frankly like this, in all good faith, and not realize that she was talking to Daniel. It was a cheap form of betrayal, Lydia thought, just like the false kiss on the bus, and she no longer wanted any part of it.

Sensing his daughter's revulsion, Daniel attempted to put a speedy end to the whole conversation.

"Those stories all date from years back, dear. You two have been divorced for ages. It's over now."

"Over?" Miranda's tea cup was swept off the chair arm as she rose. "Over? It never stops! If anything, it's worse! He's just as bad as ever, and I get no early warning signals, no control over his actions, not even the chance to tell him what I think of him afterward!"

She strode across the room. For one awful moment, Daniel thought she was coming over to hit him. But she was bending over the bookcase beside his chair.

"Over, indeed! Look what Mr. Hooper next door brought around here only a short while ago!"

She tugged at something stuck behind the bookcase.

"Look at this! Painted by my own neighbor!"

She pulled and pulled. But the painting had clearly been rammed down behind the bookcase with such force that it was difficult to remove.

Recalling only too vividly some of the unfinished

efforts Mrs. Hooper had carried home from the art class, Madame Doubtfire asked nervously:

"Are you sure this is wise, dear? In front of the children . . ."

Miranda ignored her. She was rattling the bookcase furiously. And finally out it came: Mrs. Hooper's most polished artistic achievement.

Daniel needed only the briefest of glances to feel within himself the most utter mortification. The painting was revolting. In it he stood gawky and awkward, with three out of his four limbs apparently horribly misshapen. His skin was in some places painted a rather nasty puce color, and in others a virulent cyclamen. His feet looked vile, like two deformed knobs. Worst of all he had been painted as he had modeled, stark naked.

He did try not to look. He had to look. And there, nesting within the abnormally lavish clumps of carroty undergrowth with which Mrs. Hooper had, in a generous if rather slapdash fashion, favored the lower part of his body, were his most private parts, exposed — highlighted, almost — pale, shrimpy, sad protuberances.

"My God!" he croaked, shocked beyond measure.

"Exactly!" triumphed Miranda. "What *will* people think?"

The handbag was clutched closer to the bosom in panic.

"You're not planning on *exhibiting* it, are you, dear?"

Lydia giggled.

"Why not?" she asked. "Mother should hang it over the fireplace. It's generally agreed that, after divorce, it's nice for the children to see as much as possible of their father."

Christopher fell about, laughing. Natalie looked baffled.

"It isn't funny," Miranda scolded. "It isn't funny at all. And, to cap everything, I found out this morning that I have to put up with your father playing the fool *in my own home!*"

There was a horror-struck silence. Was it possible the cat was out of the bag? Was it possible Miranda already knew?

Certainly, she was beside herself with fury.

"That's right! Look shocked! He's going to stand on this very rug, stark naked, *shameless!*"

"Am — *is* he?"

"Yes, he is! And I can't see a way to stop him. Because I was enough of a fool to promise Mrs. Hooper that if she still happened to have workmen in her house when the art college closed for half-term, her life class could meet here!"

Madame Doubtfire looked more than a little taken aback at this. She said firmly: "There must be somewhere else they could meet, dear."

Miranda scowled.

"You'd think so, wouldn't you? But it seems everyone in that class lives in either a caravan or a houseboat!" Her lip curled as she added spitefully: "Those that don't live in institutions, that is."

Daniel was bitterly regretting his ungenerous impulse at an earlier art class when volunteers were requested to offer space in their homes. He should never have claimed that he lived on a houseboat.

"So they're all coming here?"

"At ten o'clock next Tuesday morning."

Madame Doubtfire permitted her vast bosom to heave with a somewhat prudish relief as she made the best of what she perceived as the one and only bright spot in this whole boiling confusion.

"I'm very glad I don't come in till three o'clock on Tuesdays, dear. I won't have to be part of any of this."

"Oh, but you will!"

"But, dear. On Tuesday mornings I have another commitment."

"Madame Doubtfire, I'm banking on you," Miranda insisted. "I simply can't have that bunch in my house if there's no one else here on whom I can depend completely."

"But, dear. I'm not at all certain —"

Miranda interrupted the flounderings of her employee with all the firmness of the steady wage payer.

"Surely, Madame Doubtfire, it was agreed between us at the start you would be on call at other times, in case the children fell sick, or something was delivered, or the schools were on strike. There *must* be someone here. You *can't* let me down."

Madame Doubtfire was still thrashing about for an adequate and acceptable excuse for not handing out teacups at one side of the room, while standing natal bare at the other.

"But, dear, I'm not sure that I hold with nakedness . . ."

"I'm not at all surprised," Miranda said. Scornfully she indicated the painting propped up against the bookshelf. "Look at it. It's grotesque. *Grotesque!*"

She swept it up.

"In fact, I can't stand it any longer," she announced. "I'm going to put it in the garbage, where it belongs."

She could distinctly be heard adding, as she walked down the hall:

"And so does he!"

Intrigued, Lydia and Christopher looked to their father for some indication of how he intended to extricate himself from this appalling new predicament. But he was paying no attention. At Miranda's last words, his eyes had narrowed to deep slits, and drawing an imaginary catapult from one of the pockets in his voluminous tweed skirt, he edged toward the doorway and took careful aim. Once he was sure he had his former wife fully in his sights down the length of the hall, he pulled the imaginary elastic back to its farthest extent, and let fly his imaginary pebble.

When he turned around, all three children were watching him, grave-faced.

It was his eldest who finally broke the strained silence.

"Not here, Dad," Lydia chided him. Though her tone was quite even, it bore the unmistakable stamp of her mother's firmness. "Not here, in her own home. Please."

"Sorry," he told her. "Sorry, Lydia."

7

Of Acting, Happy Pigs, and War

The trip to the theater was not, in Daniel's opinion, the greatest success. By the time he remembered to pass by the theater and get tickets, the only seats still available were what the man in the box office ominously referred to as "of restricted view." But they were cheap; and still smarting from Miranda's contemptuous suggestion that he would fail to get any tickets at all, Daniel bought them anyway.

Unfortunately, the four seats were not all together. Two turned out to be behind the pillar supporting the right-hand side of the auditorium, and two behind the pillar supporting the left side. Daniel was irritated that he could not be near all three children during this rare treat, and even more irritated that this seemed to bother Lydia and Christopher so little. They moved off cheerfully, and after some argument about weak and strong eyes entailing a short series of experiments with a rolled up theater program, each chose a side of the pillar to peer around. Even before the safety curtain rose, Daniel noticed, both were staring raptly ahead.

He and Natalie did not have it so easy. Their view of the stage was restricted, not just by the vast marble column, but by a pair of fluffy-headed students. Natalie could neither see around nor over them, and as light flooded the stage set she thrashed around on her plush seat, craning for a better view. Her seat creaked horribly. Sliding across to change places, Daniel discovered that his did, too. And in the end, after prolonged sour looks from the more uncharitable of her neighbors, he felt obliged to offer Natalie a quieter perch on his own knee.

Natalie slid her arm around his neck, half throttling him. The play began. Within a minute her thumb had slid into her mouth, her eyelids were drooping, and she was twisting Daniel's hair around her fingers. Even before the first threads of the plot were established, Natalie was fast asleep. Daniel felt half inclined to wake her again — the seats were cheap, but not *that* cheap — but prudence prevailed. She lay, a dead weight in his arms, and he was forced to counterbalance with an excruciating twist of his spine if he was to see anything at all.

The play proved to be not at all suitable, Daniel thought, for family viewing. By the end he was glad Natalie had slept through the whole thing. Scene after scene of quarreling, some of it raised to quite astonishing heights of unpleasantness, unfolded a tale of two couples, one happily and one miserably married, working their way through a convoluted plot of deep-seated grudges, misunderstanding, and malice. Even the happily married couple became quite crusty under the strain of it all. But the unhappily married pair, who had been snapping at each other's kneecaps before the curtain even rose, so to speak, were dabbling in grievous bodily harm by the end of the first act.

The house lights rose. Daniel peered across the auditorium. Lydia and Christopher were sitting absolutely riveted, still staring at the curtains. It was some time before either moved a muscle. Clearly this very vivid portrayal of marital bellicosity had claimed their attention entirely. A slightly uneasy feeling crept over Daniel. In a moment of prescience he realized that staying for the rest of the play was going to prove to be a mistake.

But Natalie was still sleeping heavily in his arms, trapping him in his seat. Daniel thought Lydia and Christopher would come over during the intermission, if only to whine about ice cream. But he was mistaken. They sat without so much as turning in their seats to glance at him, their eyes fixed firmly on the safety curtain, as though fearing that the second act might start without their having noticed.

The intermission was short, the second act long. The crick in Daniel's spine was excruciating. Barrage after barrage of insult spraying from the stage reminded him of years of marriage, and made him miserable. And each time he glanced across to Lydia and Christopher and saw the silhouettes of their rapt faces, he worried himself sick about what Miranda — waspish enough after a day in Wolverhampton — would make of their account of this play for which their father had upset her sacred and inviolable weekend schedule.

At the end, Daniel's left arm and leg had lost so much feeling that he was unable to shift Natalie's weight, and rise to his feet. He sat, trapped, till Lydia and Christopher rejoined him.

"That was *magic*," breathed Christopher. "Sheer *magic*."

Magic was the most lavish of Christopher's accolades. Daniel was astonished. Turning to Lydia, he asked her:

"What did you think of it, then?"

"*Brilliant!*" Lydia was as generous with her praise as her brother. "It was the best thing I have ever seen!"

Christopher turned to stare again at the blank safety curtain.

"I don't know how the two who hated each other could even bring themselves to hold hands through that curtain call. I thought he was going to rip off her ears when she smiled at him like that, so soon after saying those terrible things!"

Daniel-the-out-of-work-actor felt the sour pang of envy. Clearly the pair on the stage had taken this part of their audience by storm.

"It's only *acting*," he muttered.

"It was easy for the other couple, though." Christopher barely registered his father's remark. "They really liked one another, you could tell."

Daniel felt irritable enough to argue.

"Of course you couldn't tell! Acting is *acting*. It's a job. For all anyone this side of the footlights knows, both couples could be married in real life. The nice pair could hate one another's guts and carry on at home like the other couple, and the quarreling pair could be bosom pals."

"Come off it, Dad!"

Even Lydia expressed skepticism.

"I'd be surprised."

The auditorium was empty now. Ushers strolled between the rows of seats, eyes peeled for abandoned umbrellas and mislaid handbags. Daniel tipped Natalie onto her feet, and held her steady while she woke.

"It's only *acting*," he repeated. "If you're an actor, you *act*. It's what you're taught to do. It's what you're paid for. You don't have to have the right feelings behind you. You simply act the part. That's what it's all about."

Neither Lydia nor Christopher responded. Both realized they had touched a raw nerve in their father. Lydia busied herself with taking Natalie's hand and leading her, still sleepy and unsteady on her feet, along the row of seats into the aisle.

Still feeling sour, Daniel followed his children out of the theater into the bright afternoon sunlight.

"That was so *good*," said Christopher again, blinking to see it was still day. "Is it time to go home now?"

Daniel had always deeply resented the implication that only Miranda's house was "home" to the children. Now he felt sufficiently irritable to push the issue.

"Home," he said. "Right. Home it is."

The children gathered to cross the road and take a bus to Springer Avenue. As though simply moving them farther along the pavement to a safer place to cross, Daniel shepherded them neatly toward the stop for his own bus. As one pulled in to the curb, he leaped aboard.

"Come on!" he encouraged them innocently from the platform. "This bus goes home."

All buses looked the same to Natalie. She climbed aboard. There was only a moment's hesitation before, not wanting to hurt his father's feelings after the treat, Christopher followed her. Lydia smothered her grimace of annoyance, and got on as well.

The bus ride was not a merry occasion. Natalie was still grumpy after her nap. The other two were getting anxious. Lydia was trying to remember exactly where Wolverhampton was, so she could work out how long her mother might have been home, waiting. Christopher was imagining the scene that would take place when Daniel finally delivered them home. It would, he decided ruefully, be rather like a third act of the play.

And it was with this still fresh in his mind that, after Daniel had unlocked the door of his apartment, and let Natalie rush between his legs to get to the television and watch the last few minutes of her favorite cartoon, Christopher turned in the hall, and said to his father:

"If it's just acting, like you said, and if you're an actor, surely you could just have acted happy and stayed in the family."

Lydia paused on her way into the living room, then dropped back to listen, pulling the door closed between the three of them and Natalie.

"Couldn't you?" Christopher challenged his father.

"Yes, I probably could," Daniel responded coldly.

He made as though to walk through to the kitchen, but Christopher didn't budge.

"If you *had*, there wouldn't have been all those terrible quarrels. You might not have had to pack up and leave."

"Possibly," Daniel admitted.

"Even back then you didn't have a regular acting job, did you?"

"No." Daniel was getting upset now.

But it seemed as if Christopher were deliberately ignoring all warning signals, for he persisted:

"So it's not as if you were busy acting all day . . ."

"All evening," Lydia corrected her brother. "Real actors act in the evening, usually."

She was just trying to lead the conversation away from the danger spot, but this unfortunate reference to "real actors" had, she suddenly realized with a sinking feeling, rubbed raw the sore of envy engendered earlier in the theater.

Christopher, however, was far too taken up with unfolding his case to pay any attention to the look in his father's eyes.

"So it's not as if you were exhausted with acting each evening. You could have acted a bit the rest of the time."

"Perhaps I could."

The tone was dangerous now, but still Christopher failed to notice.

"It wouldn't have been that hard, would it? You said yourself that it's only a job, and you don't have to have the right feelings behind you. 'You simply act the part.' That's what you said."

"Yes, I said that."

The eyes were narrowing now, and around them

was the strained, gray look that Lydia associated with her father's struggles with Miranda.

"But you didn't try that out at home?"

"No. No, I didn't."

"Christopher —" Lydia warned, but Christopher hardly heard.

"If you *had* taken the trouble to act a little at home," he was saying slowly, "then you might never have had to leave. There might not have been any separation, or any divorce, and we might all still be together as one family."

"Possibly," snapped Daniel, losing his temper. "And possibly I might be locked up in a padded cell now, screaming at the walls!"

"Why?" Christopher asked in the same false innocence with which Daniel had invited him onto the wrong bus half an hour before. "Acting's only a job, after all. You said so yourself."

Daniel took his son by the collar, squeezed hard, and slung him backward, up against the wall.

"*Because,* you little bastard," he yelled. "As you well know, a job's a job, but real life's *real!*"

Christopher held his breath, too scared even to wriggle. To Lydia, watching, it seemed forever before her father gradually loosened his fingers under Christopher's neck, let go, then shoved both hands deep in his pockets as if trying to stop himself from striking his son, hard.

Terrified, Christopher tried to back off.

"I'm sorry," he said. "I didn't mean any of that, really I didn't."

"Oh, you meant every last word of it, you little *worm!*" Daniel demolished this groveling apology. "You think I should have stayed in that damn house, day after day, week after week, year after year, living out some soul-destroying lie with your mother and just pretending it was unpaid acting work!"

"And why *not?*"

Astonishingly, this was Lydia.

Daniel stared.

"Why *not?*"

"That's right. Why not? You had us. It's your job to stick it out. You can't just knock off being a father when you decide you can't live with your wife!"

Now Daniel was beside himself with fury.

"How *dare* you?" he shouted. "*How dare you?* I never, *ever* knocked off being your father. I'm here, aren't I, rain or goddamned shine? Stuck in this god-forsaken town with no job and no prospects, just to be close to you three, just to see you a couple of times a week, keep being your damn father! I could have gone to London, you know! There's more than one theater there! I could have found work! But no, I stayed here, bored and lonely. Don't *ever* tell me again I haven't stuck at being your father, Lydia! I've been as good a father as I can!" He finished in a tone of real, deep bitterness: "As good a father as I've been allowed to be, anyhow . . ."

The anger was no longer directed at Lydia, and she knew it. And in her drive to understand, she persisted.

"But why *leave*? You said yourself you're bored and lonely. Why *not* just act, like Christopher said?"

Daniel tore at his hair.

"Because I'm a human being, that's why! Look at me! I'm *real*. I eat. I breathe. I think. I feel. I only have one life, and I want to *live* it, not act another because it fits in with less trouble. I'm not a happy pig!"

But Lydia was not to be distracted with anything so trivial as happy pigs.

"Who said anything about happy pigs? What have happy pigs to do with anything, anyway?"

At the mere mention of such strange creatures, Christopher let out a nervous giggle. He was still shaken, and he couldn't help it. Daniel spun around and, as he did so, caught a look of rising terror on his son's face. Shocked to see how one short brush with a father's considerably greater physical strength could drain away all a boy's courage, he reached out to his son, setting himself to mend the rupture between them, and settle things for all of them.

With one arm around each child, he steered them through the door into the living room, where Natalie sat hunched in front of the television, to all appearances engrossed in Extended Bowling Highlights.

Gently, he pried her fingers out of her ears.

"Fight's over, Natty," he assured her.

But the quarrel had sounded so fierce, even through the closed door, that Natalie still looked at Daniel with suspicion.

"No more getting cross with Christopher?"

"No more getting cross with Christopher."

"And no more shouting about happy pigs?"

"No, no more shouting about happy pigs."

"What *was* all that happy pig stuff, anyhow?" asked Lydia.

Daniel tried to explain.

"It's just that some things are *important*. People are prepared to suffer for them. Some feel that way about the things they do. 'Better to be a discontented poet,' said one of the great philosophers, 'than a contented pig.' "

The children thought about it.

"I *suppose* I'd think it would be better to be the poet . . ." admitted Lydia after a while.

"So would I," Christopher grudgingly agreed.

"I'd be the pig," said Natalie. "I'd definitely be the pig. I like pigs, and you said it was happy."

"But some people can't be happy unless the life they're living is real," Daniel said. "Not just an act, like on a stage, to avoid arguments and trouble. And I'm like that. Rather than go through my days acting to have a quiet life, I'd choose not to pretend, even if I end up in worse trouble."

"And everyone else does, too?"

Daniel stared at his younger daughter. Natalie, too, then. Was this the kind of thing she thought about when she sat with her fingers in her ears?

"I'm sorry," he told her. "I'm truly, truly sorry," he told all three of them.

Natalie sighed.

"Never mind," she comforted him. "It's not too bad."

"No," Christopher generously agreed. "It's not too bad."

"Lydia?"

Lydia felt it was not a father's business to fish for absolution in this way. But she was sick of the whole business. Things were as they were. To keep peace, she agreed.

"No, not too bad."

"But I am sorry, anyway . . ."

"It's all right, honestly."

"Yes."

"But —"

"But?"

"Nothing."

"*What?*" Daniel was getting edgy. "You were about to say something. What were you going to say?"

Lydia scoured the ceiling for help.

"I was just going to say that, since we have to

share in all the trouble, maybe the three of us shouldn't have to act in *our* lives, either."

"Act? You three? How?"

Lydia shrugged.

"Madame Doubtfire."

"Madame Doubtfire?"

"Yes, Madame Doubtfire." Before he could mis-understand, she rushed into an explanation. "Oh, I know that you did it for us. We've not forgotten that. But it's not *right*." She tensed her fingers, searching for the words to tell him. "It's all right for you, you see. It's like a game. You go off home at ten to seven each evening, and you can be yourself all night and all the next day till you come again. We have to stay there."

"It's difficult?"

"It's not just *difficult*," Lydia informed him. "It's almost *impossible*." She stabbed a finger meaningfully at Natalie. "Some people have even given up *trying*. And, not only that, but it isn't even *worth* it. It's not as if Madame Doubtfire is really you, after all. It's not like seeing you here, or spending time properly with you. You can't be Dad. And so it's almost as if, for all the effort you've made to buy the clothes, and make the turbans, and act it out for us, it doesn't *count*."

Daniel made as though to interrupt her, then changed his mind. Lydia went on:

"I couldn't work out what was wrong before. It didn't feel right, but I didn't know why. But maybe it's just the same problem you had, the happy pig problem. Since Madame Doubtfire isn't really you, she isn't worth so much."

"I've felt that," Christopher burst out. "*And* I don't feel as if I'm seeing much more of you, either." He shrugged. "Anyway, I prefer seeing you here, with all your —" Out of good manners, he stifled the word "mess." "With all your things."

"You still come," Daniel pointed out. "You're here now, aren't you?"

Christopher's nervousness revived.

"Yes," he said. "And we should be getting back."

"I'm sure Wolverhampton's quite close to here, really," said Lydia.

Natalie's face changed.

"Is Mother waiting for us?" she asked anxiously.

On cue, the phone began to ring.

Daniel snorted.

"Waiting, indeed! Not like your mother to wait patiently. See! Here she is, ordering you 'home.'"

He rose.

"I'll get it," he told them. "I'll show you acting finer than any you'll see in a theater." He stepped out, holding the door ajar with his heel, and hauled the phone with its cord back in the room before lifting the receiver.

The children listened to his side of the call, and had no difficulty at all imagining the other.

"*Lovely* to hear from you, Mandy. Such a sur-

prise! Thought you'd still be penned up in some Wolverhampton traffic jam. . . . What? Seven o'clock
already! *Surely* not! God, so it is. . . . Want them back
at once? Of *course* you do. It's your weekend on the
schedule, after all. . . . And no, I won't forget their
coats this time, either. . . . Yes, I quite understand.
You've driven for hours today, and don't feel like
dragging yourself out again directly. . . . Yes, I do realize that it's not your fault that I don't earn enough
nude-modeling to run a car, but I'm not quite sure I
see what. . . . *What?* You've ordered a taxi to come
around here and pick them up? And you think I
should pay for it? . . . Well, now that you mention it,
not much now, after buying all those theater tickets. . . . Yes, maybe I *should* have thought about that
sooner, but I didn't. . . . What? Not worth what? Heard
what from Mrs. Hooper? *The most unsuitable play one
could possibly have chosen for children?* Said that, did
she? Oh, dear me. . . . So sorry, Miranda. . . . Yes, Miranda. . . . Yes, Miranda. . . . Sorry, Miranda. . . .Yes,
goodbye, Miranda. . . ."

Exhausted, he held the receiver out to Lydia.

"Here, your mother wants a quick word with
you."

Lydia took the receiver, and Daniel reeled around
the room, muttering: "Yes, Miranda. . . . Agreed, Miranda. . . . Naturally, Miranda. . . . You're quite right,
Miranda. . . . Three bags full, Miranda. . . . Oh, what
a happy pig am I, Miranda. . . ."

Lydia's half of the call with her mother ran along much the same lines.

"Yes, Mother. . . . No, Mother. . . . Yes, we'll keep an eye out of the window. . . . No, I won't let him forget the coats. . . . Yes, I'll tell him. . . . No, I'll make sure he remembers. . . . No, Mother. . . . Yes, Mother. . . . Well, I quite enjoyed it, actually. Bye then, Mother. Bye."

Daniel was absolutely outraged.

"Quite enjoyed it? Quite *enjoyed* it? *'Brilliant,'* you said. *The best thing you had ever seen!*"

Christopher grinned.

"Maybe Lydia's inherited your gift for acting."

Lydia looked thoughtful.

"It's true," she said. "It wasn't a very real phone call, was it? No better than Dad's, really."

"Look on the bright side," said Christopher. "You got through it."

"Happy as a pig," said Natalie.

Only Lydia failed to smile.

"We could *all* stop."

"Stop?"

"All stop what?"

"Acting. And being happy pigs. We could all say what we really were thinking."

"If everyone did that," warned Daniel, "the world would turn into a bear garden."

"Would it?"

Natalie was fascinated. She was still sitting hugging her knees, trying to imagine a bear garden, when the taxi arrived.

Daniel pressed his last three pounds into Lydia's hand.

"I'll bring you the change next week," she assured him.

"I'll see you Monday," Daniel reminded her.

"Oh, yes! Of course!"

She ran down the stairs after the others. Daniel went to the window and threw it open. Christopher and Natalie had just dived into the taxi. Daniel called down to Lydia:

"You realize that, if you mean it, if there's to be no more acting, no more happy pigs, Madame Doubtfire will have to hand in her notice?"

Lydia waved cheerfully enough through the taxi window.

"We'll think of some other way to see a bit more of you!"

"There *is* only one other way," Daniel warned.

"What's that?"

"Tell you on Monday!" Daniel yelled.

As the taxi drew away, he slid an imaginary panel in front of him open, keyed in the three imaginary top secret codes, and waited for the imaginary silos to open.

"War," he said softly. "Total war."

And he watched his imaginary warheads making for Springer Avenue, on the horizon.

8

Funny, That's Just What Mother Always Says

Daniel spent the bus ride to Springer Avenue on Monday admiring Madame Doubtfire's letter of notice. In the back of a drawer, he had found some pale pink notepaper given to him for Christmas by Natalie a couple of years back. It was bordered with colorful, if somewhat botanically flawed, pansies. Across this paper the curvy, looping, old-fashioned handwriting he'd spent the evening practicing flowed through the equally curvy, looping, old-fashioned phrases: ". . . in accordance with our verbal undertaking to give one another two full weeks' notice . . . owing to regrettable, unforeseeable and totally unavoidable circumstances . . . cease to consider myself in your employ as from Friday week . . . must say how very much I have enjoyed the company of your absolutely charming children . . . dare to suggest they might benefit, perhaps, from a little more contact with their father . . . hope this untimely curtailment of our mutually beneficial arrangement proves not to incommode you as much as it saddens me . . . the most warm regards," and then, in the floweriest of all the signatures Daniel had contrived and the one of which he was most particularly proud:

Yours most sincerely

Euphemia D Doubtfire

Yes. No doubt about it. It was an excellent letter of notice: sensitive, firm — and inexplicable. Folding it carefully to replace it in its pansy-infested envelope, Daniel stepped off the bus, deep in thought. As soon as the children saw the letter, he knew, they would start clamoring to know Madame Doubtfire's middle name, and he was torn. Was it to be Daphnis? Deirdre? Or just plain, boring old Dolores? It was so hard to choose . . . In the middle of his reflections, the feather boa around his neck was disarranged by a fierce blast of exhaust from the departing bus. Fishing over his shoulder for floating ends, Daniel walked past next door's garden without his usual cautious survey. Mistake. For just as he turned onto Miranda's sidewalk, Mrs. Hooper pounced.

The red, round face, framed with a jumble of gray curls, rose without warning above the fence.

"Oh, Madame Doubtfire! Look at them! *Look* at them! What *can* be done?"

Forced to stop in his tracks, Daniel pocketed Madame Doubtfire's letter of notice, lifted his skirts, and picked his way across the muddy flower beds to where Mrs. Hooper stood, pointing to something in her own garden.

"Oh, Madame Doubtfire, what *do* you think?"

Daniel peered over. It wasn't at all clear to which particular horticultural disaster she was referring; and Daniel, frankly, didn't much care. There was a deep fund of resentment within him against this old neighbor. She had caused him a good deal of trouble recently. First, that abysmal and offensive painting. He'd not forgive her easily for that. Then this appalling mix-up with the art class. He still hadn't worked out how he was going to manage to be two people at once all tomorrow morning. And, on top of everything, those quite unsolicited remarks to Miranda about the unsuitability of the play he'd chosen for the children. They hadn't gone down at all well.

He reached up and straightened his turban against the sharp breeze.

"Is that canker I spy on your prunus?" he cooed.

"Canker? On my prunus?" Mrs. Hooper looked anxious. "No, I don't think so."

"I wasn't saying it *was*," Madame Doubtfire assured her. "I was only suggesting it *might* be. It only *looks* as if it is. And then, one does so often find it flourishing where there are other garden diseases . . ."

"Other garden diseases?"

Daniel noted with satisfaction that Mrs. Hooper's face had turned just a little bit redder, and her tone of voice a shade less confiding and neighborly. He pressed home his advantage.

"Well — yes, dear. Not that I'm an expert . . ." Madame Doubtfire shrugged in a modest, self-deprecating fashion that both gave Mrs. Hooper to understand clearly that she was, and sent the feather boa slithering uncontrollably down her back into the wallflowers. "But all the other neighbors have mentioned often enough, over the fence, how you have had your little problems . . ."

"Little problems?"

The face was very red indeed, now.

"Oh, nothing serious! Nothing serious at all!" At the very idea of the diseases being serious, Madame Doubtfire gave a little laugh. "Just the rust on your hollyhocks, dear. And the club root on your brussels sprouts. The mildew over your gooseberries. That crown gall that spoils your roses . . ."

Mrs. Hooper turned turkey-wattle scarlet with rage. She was so angry, she was speechless.

"Nothing important at all," Madame Doubtfire soothed. "Nothing at all. Though Mr. Fairway has mentioned once or twice that on your spuds last year there was some very nasty blackleg."

"Now look at the pot calling the kettle black!" cried Mrs. Hooper, galvanized back into speech by sheer outrage. "When everyone in the street knows that Mr. Fairway has carrot root fly!"

But Madame Doubtfire was picking her way delicately back through the mud to the safety of the flagstone walk.

"Does he, dear?" she asked vaguely, over her shoulder. "I must say that I hadn't noticed." She shook mud from her skirts before stepping onto the porch. "Though, now you come to mention it, I did hear tell he had a touch of rheumatism . . ."

And leaving Mrs. Hooper hopping, she disappeared inside.

Where Daniel had planned to leave his note, propped up against the flower vase on the hall table, there was another waiting. It was stapled to two ten-pound notes, so Daniel read it. From the quality of the handwriting, it was apparent Miranda had written it in a great hurry.

He read aloud: "Please find time, if you can, to

buy Natalie jeans — hardy, machine-washable, room for growth, and *not white*. Thank you. Miranda."

"Not white" was underlined four times.

"Seems very reasonable," Daniel told the spider plant. "One pair of jeans. Shouldn't cause a lot of problems."

He took it easy until Natalie came home from school: strolled around the house watering the plants that he now considered to be more his than Miranda's; telephoned a number of acting agencies in the hope of hearing of possible openings; took off his feather boa and turban, and, tilting back his chair, sat with his feet on the kitchen table, drinking a cup of coffee and chatting to Hetty, trying to coax a bit more life into her.

The quail was looking terribly unhappy, he thought. She sat hunched unresponsively in the corner of her cage, with her head at a curious and uncomfortable-looking angle. Even when he whistled at her, she barely blinked. Tiny gray molted feathers were scattered all over the cage floor, and her plumage looked drab. This was by no means the fat and glossy Hetty of good health and spirits. She peeped only now and again, softly and mournfully. From time to time, her little body shivered.

Daniel sat trying to work out how old she was. Christopher, he recalled, had brought her home from the pet shop the summer before that last great series of battles with Miranda that led to the final separation.

Daniel remembered quite clearly hurling a teapot at
the kitchen wall in a fury of frustration, and seeing
Hetty get showered with cold, wet tea leaves. So she
was nearly four, at least. Getting on, for a quail. And
no one knew quite how old she had been when Christopher bought her.

So, thought Daniel, watching the poor creature
look so miserable in the corner of her cage, this was
in all likelihood extreme old age. And since for that
there was no cure but endurance, he simply did what
little he could to make her a bit more comfortable.
Switching on the oven to the temperature for gently
drying out meringues, Daniel moved Hetty's cage
closer, to keep her warm. He scrubbed her water dish
till it was scrupulously clean, refilled it, and pushed
it nearer. He peeled a few delicacies from Miranda's
vegetable rack, diced them, and laid them beside her.
She took no interest in them at all, and he was still
watching her anxiously when the front door banged,
taking him entirely by surprise.

Daniel dived for his turban and feather boa. Could
it be three fifteen already? Surely not! But here was
Natalie, pushing open the kitchen door while a flus-
tered Daniel was still tugging the swirling golden turban over the hair above his ears.

"Heavens! You *are* back early, dear!"

In his haste, he tugged too hard, snapping the
bar of the poodle brooch that held the folds of lurid
material in place. The turban fell apart, and layer

after layer of gold flannelette tumbled down over his face and shoulders, blinding and nearly strangling him.

"Oh, s — *ugar!*" swore Daniel, desperately clawing through the tangles.

Unable even to wait until he had fully extricated himself, Natalie thrust something in his hand.

"Read that, Dad!" she ordered proudly.

Under the circumstances, with folds of gold turban ignominiously wreathed around his neck, there seemed to Daniel little point in insisting on being Madame Doubtfire. So he read out, in his own voice:

> " 'It is the intention of this circular to acquaint all parents of Midkelvin Region schoolchildren with the arrangements for immediate strike action decided upon at yesterday's meeting of the combined unions.' "

— oh, not *again!*"

"Not *that* side," Natalie complained. "That's just old scrap. Look on the *other* side!"

Daniel turned the sheet of paper over, and tried again. He started with the title, in huge, thick, laboriously penciled letters.

Egogs.

"*Hedge*hogs," Natalie corrected him, hurt.

"Sorry. *Hedgehogs*." He read on.

> I followed a really smelly one up our path. It sneezed.

He lowered the sheet of paper and stared at Natalie. "Sneezed? Really? A hedgehog?"

Natalie nodded.

"It kept on sneezing," she assured him gravely. "Right up the path."

Amused, Daniel swept his small daughter up into his arms. "Well, well!" he said. "Quite the naturalist, aren't we?"

"Go *on!*" insisted Natalie, struggling in his arms. She was getting impatient.

Daniel put her down, and read further.

> Miss Coates thinks there are no egogs in the Mrs Sippy River.

He raised an eyebrow.

"How do you *know?*"

"I asked her."

"But why ask about the Mississippi River, in particular?"

Natalie sighed.

"It's the only river I know, except for The Looking Glass River in my book. And we're always singing songs about it at school."

Shaking his head in wonder, Daniel read on.

Egogs have fleas. We do not have them in our house. But we do have a qu

Here, the report on hedgehogs came to an abrupt end.

"The bell rang," Natalie explained. "While I still had my hand up."

"Hand up?"

"For quail."

"To spell it? Or to check if there are any in the Mississippi River?"

Natalie ignored this, and Daniel turned the page back over to the circular on immediate strike action. He felt a little more sympathetic, reading it through this second time.

"Jeans," he informed Natalie over the top. "We're off to buy you jeans."

"My socks are wet."

"Hop up and change them, Natalie."

She hopped upstairs. He heard the floorboards shake all the way up, watched the ceiling quiver as she hopped across the landing, then heard, overhead, one last sickening thud that made the light fittings rattle. There was silence. He understood her to be sitting quietly in front of her chest of drawers, looking for a clean, dry pair of socks.

For no accountable reason, Daniel found himself wondering if Miranda kept any aspirin in her bathroom cabinet.

The front door banged again. It was Christopher and Lydia this time.

"What's for tea?"

"I'm *starving*."

Lydia threw her schoolbag on to the floor, where Daniel promptly tripped over it.

"Pick that *up*, Lydia."

Lydia made a face.

"Sor-ree!" she sang. "What happened to your turban? It looks all funny."

Ignoring her, Daniel scoured the shelf of cookbooks for something different. He was thoroughly sick of cooking, frankly. What had once been a real pleasure — preparing nice meals to delight his children on their visits — had become nothing but a daily grind and a bore. He'd reached the stage of stirring malignant thoughts into his efforts; and he reckoned if he had to make stuffed bread one more time, for anyone, he'd put arsenic in it instead of garlic.

He pried down from the overloaded shelf a book he hadn't looked at in years, not since the earliest days of his marriage. It was called the *Alphonse Lamarquier Cook Book*. Perhaps there was something quick and simple in this one. It had to be quick because he and

Natalie still had to go out and buy jeans; and it had to be simple because he was close to being driven out of his mind with chop, chop, chop and scrape, scrape, scrape, with grate, grate, grate and sizzle, sizzle, sizzle.

The *Alphonse Lamarquier Cook Book* fell open at chapter four — Soups. *To slaughter a turtle,* Daniel read, *lay it on its back on a table with its head hanging over the side.* His eyes traveled down the page, passing more quickly over the paragraph on the correct dismemberment of the turtle, and the sections on the preparation of the carapace, the plastron and the flippers.

He shut the book.

"Cheese on toast?" he suggested.

"Oh, not again!"

"We're *always* having cheese on toast."

"Did you get any of the cheese I like? If you didn't, I don't think I want any cheese on toast, thank you."

Daniel glared at them both.

"I wonder if Alphonse Lamarquier had to put up with this."

"Who?"

"Put up with *what?*"

"Nothing. No one." Once again, Daniel found himself thinking about aspirin. "Why don't you two just get started quietly on your homework?"

"I can't do mine quietly," triumphed Lydia. "It's oboe practice!"

As Christopher unloaded the detritus of his

schoolbag on to the table, looking for his geography book, Lydia sent everything cascading out of a cupboard on to the floor, searching for her oboe.

Daniel reached up to the very top shelf in the small pantry and laid his fingers on two cans of tomato soup. He felt defeated and a little guilty, remembering with some embarrassment the day he first came to work for Miranda and noticed the cans hidden away up there at the back in the corner; and disapproved of them to himself, convinced in his own mind that he himself would never be reduced to feeding his children such uninspired fare.

Christopher picked up a pen. It never occurred to him to give the homework any thought of his own. His father was standing there, and so he asked him:

"How do we waste most energy in Britain?"

"Heat loss," Daniel responded automatically. "British homes have deplorable insulation."

Christopher's pen raced. He knew when he was on to a good thing.

"Which countries do have properly insulated homes?"

"Norway," Daniel suggested. "Norwegian houses are thoroughly well insulated. Light a match, and the whole house is boiling."

"Fart, and you've got a heat wave."

"Christopher!"

"Sorry."

Christopher lay low. Lydia started up.

"I can't work out the key signature," she complained.

"Just practice it anyway," ordered Daniel.

Lydia was outraged.

"How can I practice it if I don't know what key it's in? I don't know which notes to play, do I? So I can't play it."

"There are the notes." Daniel pointed irascibly to the music. "Just play those, can't you?"

"Sure!" Lydia snapped. "Fine! Just so long as you tell me, as I go along, which ones are sharps and which are flats!"

Daniel retreated hastily to the stove.

"It's no use asking *me*," he defended himself, stirring madly. "All music looks like daffodils growing along a roadside to me. Thickly or thinly planted, it's all daffodils to the average grade one recorder player."

Lydia blew a ferocious blast through her oboe. Daniel jumped out of his skin. The spoon flew out of the soup pan, and spattered orange stains all down the front of Madame Doubtfire's frock.

"Lydia! Go off and practice somewhere else!"

Still blowing a fiendish noise through her oboe, Lydia strolled out.

Daniel was just cherishing the silence when Christopher broke it. He tipped another load of clutter on to the table, this time in search of his math book.

"Why do we have to learn about fractions, anyway?" he groused.

"Fractions are useful," Daniel told his son. "Nobody ever gets all they want out of life."

And he was still standing, stirring the soup, reflecting on a few less than perfect wholes in his own existence, when from beside the oven came a pathetic little cheep.

Christopher looked up, startled, from his homework.

"Was that Hetty?"

He looked around, and saw the stool on which the cage usually rested.

"Where is she? Where have you put the cage?"

"Down here."

Daniel touched Hetty's cage with his foot.

"Why did you move it?"

"See for yourself."

Christopher came over. He peered through the cage bars at his pet.

"She looks a bit funny."

Gently, Daniel attempted to raise the subject of Hetty's condition.

"I don't think she's at all well . . ."

"Poor Hetty. Maybe she needs company. Maybe she ought to have a baby."

"I think she's a little too old to be having any babies . . ."

"Anyhow, we'd need another quail's help."

"I'm afraid she's well past all that as well now, Christopher."

Daniel was trying; but his son was determined to block out the message hidden beneath his father's words.

"If Hetty will pardon the expression" — Christopher grinned and tapped the cage bars — "the whole idea's enough to make her quail!"

"Christopher —"

But his son still refused to hear what he was saying.

"You'd like some babies, wouldn't you, Hetty?" Christopher crooned.

Daniel's patience gave way in the face of this stubborn insistence that here was a broody, not a dying quail.

"Pity it's not the right time of year," he snapped sarcastically. "You could convince yourself that she was only going into hibernation."

And switching off the gas beneath the soup, he stormed upstairs to root out Natalie.

She was still sitting beside her chest of drawers, looking forlorn. A sea of socks surrounded her.

"For God's sake, Natalie! How long does it take you to put on one dry pair of socks?"

Natalie scowled.

"I haven't got a pair."

"Don't be ridiculous!"

"*You* look," she challenged him. "I can't find two the same anywhere."

Furious, Daniel rooted through the mess on the floor. To his annoyance, Natalie was right. Socks there were in profusion; but not one pair.

"Well, where are all the others?" he demanded.

"Over at your house," Natalie said.

"Oh, *God!*"

Gritting his teeth, he dived down and picked out two socks — one knee-length blue, and one short and green.

"Here! Put on these! We have to *go*, Natalie. It's half past four already."

"We could buy them tomorrow."

Daniel considered. But tomorrow, he knew today, would be an awful day from start to finish.

"We're going *now*. We have two whole hours."

Thinking about it afterward, Daniel could not for the life of him work out where those two whole hours went. Admittedly, they went to several shops. The first had no jeans at all, and the second only white ones. The third had jeans in red and blue and apple green, but they were labeled *Caution: wash separately*, so Daniel, remembering Miranda's firm specifications, was forced to pry a wistful and somewhat resentful Natalie away. The fourth shop had machine-washable jeans in gray, but not in Natalie's size. The fifth had four pairs of jeans in Natalie's size, but none of them fit. Nor did those labeled with the size above, nor the size above that.

"They *pinch*," Natalie grumbled, pulling irritably at the crotch. "They're too tight here. They *hurt*."

"Have you tried Notweeds?" asked the saleslady, coldly.

So they tried Notweeds. As they approached its wide glass frontage, two young sales clerks standing on the other side broke off their avid gossiping to stare in wonder at the sight of this extraordinary Amazon, with dappled makeup and tufts of hair shooting from her most peculiar headgear, her bosom richly splashed with tomato soup stains, her skirt mud-rimmed, leading by the hand the most fetching child imaginable, wearing odd socks.

As the glass doors swung open, the girls sprang to life.

"We're closing now," they chanted in unison.

The braver of the two laid her hand on the sleeve of Madame Doubtfire's cardigan, to shoo her out.

Daniel was irritated. Drawing himself up to full height, he towered over the girl, and thundered:

"Young lady, the notice affixed to that door says plainly that you close at half past five."

"It's practically that now," the girl argued.

"There are still seven minutes left."

"That isn't really long enough to try anything for size."

"Then we shall *look*."

"There isn't much point," persisted the girl. The expression on her face said clearly that nothing for sale in this shop would ever fit someone Madame Doubtfire's size.

"Come, Natalie," said Daniel. "You'd like to look at all these lovely clothes, wouldn't you?"

"No," Natalie said. "I want to go home."

The clerk made the mistake of smirking.

"Tough!" Daniel told Natalie. "For we are looking anyway, for seven whole minutes."

"Six, now," the clerk corrected insolently.

Natalie practically had to be dragged between the racks of clothes. She trailed her feet along the floor so stubbornly, she left tracks even on the hardy shop carpet. She was horribly fractious, complaining loudly and bitterly: her feet were hurting; her legs ached; she wanted to go home; she was missing "Sesame Street"; she didn't even *like* jeans.

"We don't stock them anyway," crowed the sales clerk.

She was quite right. The entire children's section comprised no more than two short racks of clothes, and one of these was almost bare. Neither contained jeans of any description, and even sorting through as slowly as possible, Daniel only managed to exhaust a further minute and a half.

"Four minutes."

The girl's voice was thick with spite.

"Can't we go *ho-ome?*"

Natalie's pitiful wail would have melted the heart of a Nero. But Daniel was made of sterner stuff.

"We'll go when I say so, Natalie. Not before."

They moved between the racks, with Daniel trying to pretend he wasn't having to tug at Natalie's arm quite as sharply as he was, nor threaten her so continuously under his breath.

"Two minutes!"

Daniel lifted a dress from the rack beside him, and shuddered. Really, some of these clothes were an embarrassment! Clearly, in this shop the order of the day was bare backs, bare midriffs and — shrinking back in horror — bare fronts. How could today's girls dress in such scandalous garments? How come they didn't catch their deaths of cold? And how could *anyone* be thin enough to get in that one?

"I can't *walk* anymore. I'm *tired*."

"One minute!"

The girls stood side by side next to the doors, hate in their eyes, keys jangling. Daniel inspected the nighties.

Outside, the clock in the church tower embarked upon its half-hour chime. Seizing Natalie more tightly by the hand, Daniel swept past the glowering girls.

"Thank you, my dears," he said, inclining his head in a most gracious fashion. "You've been so helpful."

Only as the door swung closed behind did he hear, wafted out on the draft:

"What a *cruel woman!*"

Outside, and on the spot, Natalie recovered totally.

"Can we go on to Barton's now?" she begged. "Barton's doesn't close till six. They have an ice-cream stand outside."

"No, dear," said Daniel. "Madame Doubtfire's exhausted. We'll go home now."

"But what about my jeans? Shall we come back and try again tomorrow?"

"No!" Daniel shuddered. "I don't think so, dear. Shopping for clothes after school is altogether impossible. It's much more sensible to leave the whole business till there's more time at the weekend."

"Funny," said Natalie, slipping her hand in his as they set off for home along the street. "That's just what Mother always says."

9

The Day of the Storm Is Not a Day for Thatching

The next day was, as he had feared, an awful day from start to finish. When Daniel turned up for work at Springer Avenue in his clean dress and a nice fresh turban, he was appalled to find his three children waiting excitedly for him.

"Why aren't you all in school?" he demanded.

"Strike," Lydia said. "There was a note about it yesterday."

"Nobody showed *me* any note about a strike."

"Natalie showed you hers. We saw it lying on the kitchen table. That's why we didn't bother to give you ours."

Daniel was adamant.

"I saw no note."

"You *must* have," Lydia insisted. "*We* saw it. There was some drivel about hedgehogs written all over the back."

Light dawning, Daniel spun around and accused his younger daughter.

"You told me that was just an *old scrap*."

Natalie was tearful. Lydia's careless remark about drivel had hurt her feelings.

"I got mixed up."

Daniel sighed.

"Never mind. It doesn't make any difference. Here you are, anyway." Then a thought struck him. The blood drained from his cheeks, leaving Madame Doubtfire's *Apricot Crème* foundation looking like cheap gold leaf on the face of a corpse. "Yes, it *does* make a difference! You can't stay here! *None* of you! Not today!"

"Why not?"

The blood helter-skeltered back. Now Daniel's face was positively puce.

"Because the art class is on its way over here later this morning. And I'm supposed to be standing on that rug over there, stark naked!"

"We don't mind," all the children assured him kindly.

"*I* mind. I mind a *lot*."

"We've often seen you with no clothes," Lydia comforted her father. "We saw you the time that London theater phoned while you were in the bath, and when you laid insulation in the loft and Mother made you put every stitch you were wearing into a plastic bag before you climbed down."

"And when your towel fell off at Llandudno," Natalie said. "Everyone on the beach saw you that time."

"This is quite different," Daniel told them. "I am no prude. The odd fleeting glimpse of my bare bottom? Fine by me! The washcloth placed for modesty in the bathtub floating away as the attention wanders? No embarrassment! But standing stone still for three hours on the hearth rug in my birthday suit, with my own children watching? No, thank you! No, no, no!"

The children all looked horribly disappointed. None of them spoke. After a moment's strained silence, Daniel asked them:

"Isn't there somewhere you can go and *play?*"

"*Play?*"

"*Play?*"

Lydia and Christopher's voices made their contempt for this idea perfectly plain.

"*Read,* then. Paint? Cook?" Daniel was getting desperate. "If I gave you some money, you could go shopping."

"How much money?"

Daniel fished in the pockets of Madame Doubtfire's dress. But the money Miranda had left for Natalie's jeans the day before had, he now realized, gone to the cleaners in the soup-stained skirt.

Daniel despaired.

"Oh, I give *up!*"

With all the raw cunning of youth, each child immediately affected to interpret this as permission to stay at home and watch the show. Rather than risk any change of mind on their father's part, they fled upstairs, pretending they didn't hear when he called them back, determined they would be all he could wish — good as gold, silent as mice — until the glorious, promised moment.

Daniel rushed into the kitchen. He had scarcely had time to plug in the kettle and lay out coffee cups and have a quick peep into Hetty's cage — she was looking, if possible, even more bedraggled and dispirited than the day before — when the doorbell rang. It was Mrs. Hooper.

Wiping his hands on his apron, Daniel attempted to block the doorway.

"You're rather early for the art class, I'm afraid, dear. Nobody else has arrived yet, and —"

Using her easel as a battering ram, Mrs. Hooper pushed past. Behind her, Daniel could see two other members of the art class already struggling off the bus with their portfolios and folding easels.

Sighing, he left the front door ajar, and followed Mrs. Hooper through to the kitchen.

Caught in the act of helping herself to coffee, Mrs. Hooper smiled ingratiatingly.

"I'll just pour ours, shall I, Madame Doubtfire?"

"Make it four, dear," said Daniel. "The others are coming."

First four cups, then six, then seven, then eleven. Daniel suffered the endless round of polite introductions as one member of the art class after another arrived, and stood fretting in Miranda's kitchen.

"Where can Mr. Hilliard be?"

"It's not like him to be late."

"I *gave* him the address."

"You'd think he might phone . . ."

"I'm sure he's on his way right now."

Cue for my entrance, thought Daniel. Nodding and smiling at them all as pleasantly as possible, he sidled toward the door armed with the sugar bowl, offering lumps, and planning to sneak upstairs and change quickly, then materialize at the front door as himself. But suddenly, in the doorway, the crucial flaw in this simple plan presented itself in all its hideous clarity. He had no clothes! He had forgotten to bring his trousers with him! He had no jacket, no shirt, no socks! He was right up the creek!

"What on earth can have happened?"

"Where *is* he?"

"It's too bad, really. He should have phoned."

"It's really quite late. We should have started twenty minutes ago."

With absolutely no alternative in view, Daniel took the plunge.

"Finished your coffee, everyone?" he cooed, in

Madame Doubtfire's most motherly way. "Shall I take your cups, dears? You all go in the front room and set up your nice easels and lay out your pencils, and I'll call Mr. Hilliard for you."

"Call Mr. Hilliard? Is he *here?*"

"Has he been hiding all this time?"

"Not *hiding*, dears. He just arrived a little early, and slipped out into the garden for a smoke."

Around him, Daniel heard rebellious whispers.

"Here? All this time!"

"The woman might have had the sense to mention it before!"

"Didn't she hear us worrying? Is she *deaf?*"

"I didn't know that Mr. Hilliard smoked."

Forgetting himself for a moment, Daniel responded to the last remark.

"I do enjoy an occasional cheroot."

Everyone turned to stare. Madame Doubtfire wasn't their picture of an occasional cheroot smoker; but, then again, they wouldn't have thought, either, that she was stone deaf.

Panicking, Daniel ushered them hastily out of the kitchen.

"Off you go, dears. You settle yourselves down nicely in the front room, and in less time than it takes for you to unpack all your lovely cadmium yellows and cobalt blues, Mr. Hilliard will be standing in front of you, I promise."

Still grumbling a little ungraciously among themselves about the foolish and unnecessary delay, the members of the art class began to shuffle through the hall, carrying their folders and equipment.

Daniel fled up the stairs. Christopher was waiting on the landing.

"Can we come down now?"

"Certainly not!"

Daniel pushed his son before him in to Miranda's bedroom.

"Quick," he said. "Root through your mother's wardrobe while I get undressed, and find something I can wrap around me."

"What sort of something?"

"I don't know!" Daniel tore off his dress. "Something to distract them. Something colorful — a challenge to paint!"

"How about this?"

Christopher held up a rainbow-colored sweater stamped with an anti-nuclear symbol.

"God, no! I couldn't stand the arguing. Find something else!"

As Daniel wiped off Madame Doubtfire's *Apricot Crême* Foundation Christopher held up a pair of frilly French panties spangled with sweet little heart shapes.

"How about these?"

"No!"

"You'll have to wear this wrap, then. It's all I can find."

Daniel stepped away from Madame Doubtfire's

clothing, which lay in a heap on Miranda's carpet, reeking gently of lavender. Christopher handed him a richly patterned paisley shawl with scarlet tassels.

"Oh, all *right!*"

Daniel wrapped the shawl around his torso, and knotted it.

"Careful," warned Christopher. "That's one of Mother's favorite things. You'll be in trouble if you spoil it."

"The woman's out for my blood already."

"She certainly is," grinned Christopher. "You should have heard what she was saying last night about you modeling for the art class in this house. 'Thank heaven you three will all be safely away in school,' she kept saying. We didn't dare let on there was a strike. We all left for school as usual this morning, and hid in the garden until she'd gone."

Daniel was horrified.

"Suppose she comes back! She could easily. She'll have received my resignation this morning. She might rush back home to try to persuade me to stay after all."

"If she comes back, you'll be a dead man."

"Oh, God!" cried Daniel.

And, tassels flying, he ran downstairs.

Downstairs was little better, for his entrance provoked a storm of argument. One body of aesthetic opinion was that he should stand in natural daylight from the window with his colorful paisley loincloth hanging free. Another school of thought held he should sit in lamplight, with the paisley showing to advantage in soft folds. ("See how the red *speaks* to the mauve!" cried Dr. Hamid quite excitedly.) Mrs. Hooper's suggestion that he remove his paisley shawl entirely was courteously ignored by everyone present.

Daniel stepped on the hearthrug, and perched rather delicately on a stool. The wood was cold on his bare bottom. For a minute or two he did try to accommodate their various requests and suggestions.

"Could you turn your face just the tiniest smidgeon to the left? Thank you. Quite perfect!"

"Is it possible for you to extend your foot — so!"

"Are we agreed that the left arm should hang in that fashion?"

But gradually he stopped responding to their remarks altogether, making it plain he considered himself settled. Like it or lump it, this was today's pose.

And most of them liked it. Cramped though they were in these far from ideal surroundings, they rooted contentedly in their little boxes for crayons and charcoal, for pencils and pastels. After the first few waves of soft apologies — "*So* sorry." "Can you still see now I've shifted a little?" "Whoops!" "Did *I* knock that? I do apologize!" — companionable silence reigned, broken only by the occasional restrained grunt of happy accomplishment or, more often, frustration, and Miss Purkett's short bursts of classical humming.

Daniel relaxed. The stool warmed up. Perhaps

it wasn't going to be so bad after all. Indeed, he could almost begin to envisage picking his way through the morning without a disaster. If only the children had the sense and restraint to stay quietly upstairs, out of the way . . . If only no one drifted off prematurely in search of that nice Madame Doubtfire and a spot more hot coffee . . . If only Miranda had a series of recalcitrant problems to keep her safely installed at the Emporium . . .

A whole hour passed. Scatch, scrape, rub, hum. It was all rather soothing, really. Such were the heights of Daniel's restored optimism that he was actually enjoying himself, sitting quite happily and complacently, and relishing the fact, as it struck him, that he was earning double wages. He even began to wonder if he might not dare suggest a short break — rush upstairs, thrust himself back in his dress and his turban, plaster a little *Apricot Crème* foundation over his cheeks, and sail down the stairs to preside over coffee while "Mr. Hilliard" perhaps tactfully disappeared along the road in search of more cheroots and another quiet smoke?

But there's no armor against fate. While he was comfortably sitting there, consciously having to restrain himself from swinging his legs, and idly trying to invent some feasible explanation for how a grown man in a loincloth could disappear from view in seconds flat on a suburban street, Daniel's line of vision drifted momentarily toward the garden. And there he saw for the first time, dotted like little planted heads in pots between the geraniums on the windowsill, his own three children staring in at him, and, right behind them, rushing up the path like one of the Furies, his former wife.

"Dear gods!" Daniel cried inwardly. "Save, save me now!"

He couldn't bear to look. There was no need. Even as he sat outwardly so composed on his stool, looking the other way, he could see easily in his mind's eye her glare of withering disapproval through the glass, feel the swatting hands, imagine without difficulty the furious, whispered admonition: "Get *down!* Away from that window this *minute,* all three of you! Why aren't you in school? What? A *strike?* Nobody said a word to *me!* And where is Madame Doubtfire? Why has she left you without supervision, today of all days!"

His eyes cautiously swiveled right, just for a moment. The garden was empty. He thought he heard the back door bang, and, seconds afterward, a series of scuffles up the staircase. Miranda must be herding them upstairs, poor little mites, for one of her thorough tongue-lashings, in private.

He couldn't bear it. He leaped off his stool.

"Excuse me," he cried. "Back in a moment!"

And leaving them staring, he ran out of the room.

*   *   *

They met on the stairs. He stopped and looked up. She was coming down. Her expression was puzzled, and in her hand was his flowery turban, looking for all the world as innocent as some bright tea cosy, as inoffensive as any little household object carried downstairs.

"Where's Madame Doubtfire?"

"Miranda —"

The look of bewilderment intensified. She stared at him with narrowed eyes. She sniffed the air. Was it the careless streak of *Apricot Crème* below his hairline that gave him away? Or his faint, trailing smell of lavender?

Whichever it was, the game was up. Miranda knew.

"You're Madame Doubtfire!"

"Miranda! Listen —"

"You're Madame Doubtfire! All the time!"

"Miranda! Please! I can explain!"

The turban caught him hard, full in the face. And, just like all the others, the battle began.

"How *dare* you?" Miranda shook with rage. "How *dare* you deceive me like this, and arrange for my own children to deceive me? How *dare* you encourage them to collude with you in lying to me and humiliating me?"

Faced with this barrage of self-righteousness, Daniel's apprehension promptly turned into anger.

"You get straight off your high horse, Miranda, before it throws you! Before you start criticizing me, try asking yourself who reduced all of us to deceiving you this way! Ask yourself how a father can end up forced to disguise himself to get to see his own damn children! Ask yourself why those same children agreed to go along with the plan in the first place! If you don't care for what we've done, you try remembering it's only your selfishness and thoughtlessness and lack of consideration for everyone else's wishes and feelings that started this whole thing in the first place!"

"You saw them regularly! I never stopped you!"

"You never helped me, either. Ever since the divorce, you've treated me like some inconvenient leftover! If I saw them, it was in *spite* of you!"

"What do you mean, 'in *spite* of' me? Even if I was exhausted after work, even if I was *dropping*, I drove them over to you every week."

"*Hours* late."

"So sometimes I'm late! Well, I do have a job, you know. Unlike you. For fourteen years I've been the only steady breadwinner in this family. I work damn hard. You don't know what that means. Perhaps you should. You don't like me turning up at that squalid, messy apartment of yours a few minutes later than expected; but I notice you don't actually make the effort to get a job so you can run a car and pick them up yourself! If the alternative's work, boring hard *work* — work like mine that means half the time

coming home too tired to speak to them *anyway* —
maybe you're not as keen as you make out to see all
you can of your sweet little darlings!"

The sweet little darlings concerned sat listening
in a row, whey-faced, as though caged behind the
banister bars. Christopher had begun to hum very
softly, his thin, tuneless humming of trapped distress.
Downstairs, behind Daniel, the members of the art
class were creeping silently out of the house, one by
one, with their faces averted and their heads bowed.

"I'm *warning* you, Miranda," Daniel said dangerously. "Don't you dig that old chestnut up again!
You were glad enough in the old days to have me
slopping around the kitchen looking after sick babies
when you went charging out to the Emporium in your
smart suit and fancy shoes! Don't try and taunt me
now for my lack of a job!"

"Why not?" She was far too angry herself to be
intimidated by his anger. "Why *not*? *My* personality
seems to be on the agenda! Why shouldn't yours?
You're lazy, poor and irresponsible. You always have
been and you always will be. But I never thought you'd
sink so low as to take my hard-earned money from
me as wages for cheating, and lying, and nosing round
my house uninvited, and making a perfect fool of me
in front of my own children!"

"I took your money in return for doing a job
you wanted done. *And* I did it well. You said so often
enough yourself! And I'd have been happy to do it

without taking any money at all, or lying and making a fool of you, if you'd had the sense and consideration to let me look after them after school when I asked you!"

"I was quite right not to trust you with them, wasn't I? You've just proved *that*. I knew that you were irresponsible, but I did think you had some small amount of sensitivity. How sensitive is it, Daniel Hilliard, to have a job unknown to your ex-wife that involves rummaging through her underwear, and deciding what needs to go into the laundry basket!"

Daniel rammed his fist, hard, against the wall.

"There you go," he scoffed. "There you go again! That's always been your trouble, Miranda! All you can ever see is how other people have wronged you! It never occurs to you you might have wronged them first, or driven them to it!"

"Oh, *I* drove you to this, did I?" Her voice was venomous. "I drove you to this? I drove you into handing me cups of tea and encouraging me to talk freely about our marriage with all three children sitting there, listening, knowing who you were *all the time*." Her voice dropped to a whisper. "You've made such a fool of me, Daniel Hilliard. And you think you have some *excuse*?"

Gripping the banister, she leaned her head down and almost spat at him.

"What you have done is unforgivable. *Unforgiv-*

able! I won't forgive you for it, *ever!* And the children will understand — won't you?"

She swung around to them in appeal. None of them moved. None of them spoke. Their faces were pale little masks. Even the humming had stopped now.

Daniel appealed to them in his turn.

"Tell her! *Tell* her, damn you! Tell her how all this began only because she was so impossible, so blind to your wishes and to mine, because she was always totally *deaf* to any suggestion that inconvenienced her, even for a moment, that '*disrupted her routine.*' " He spat the expression out like a bad taste. "Tell her that you three only agreed because she was always so stubborn, so sure that whatever suited *her* best was good for everybody else!"

"I *will* not have you speak to the children about me like this in my own house!"

"Why not?" He gave out a very nasty sounding laugh, and spun around dramatically. "Why *not?* You denigrate me *continually* in this house! Don't forget I've been here, and. I've heard you! I've heard the things you say about me!" He pointed a finger at her threateningly. "And they have to listen. Oh, yes. But you don't know what they're thinking, do you, Miranda? You don't realize that to them it only shows your rotten judgment in marrying me in the first place, your ungenerous nature, and your tiny mind! You do yourself no favors when you bad-mouth me. You simply force them to hide their affection for their father from you." The finger waggled warningly from side to side. "And you're on very dangerous ground here, Miranda. Very dangerous indeed. Because no one can easily hide their feelings from someone they love, and if you force them to hide enough from you, they'll simply stop loving you as much, so they can keep their little secret more easily!"

"They'll never stop loving me! I am their *mother!*"

"And they'll never stop loving me, either! I am their *father!*"

There was so much hate between them that each was silenced.

Lydia rose. Her rage lent her an ashen, fierce dignity that neither parent had seen before.

"I hate you *both,*" she informed them in an unsteady voice, and, turning, she walked into her bedroom and shut the door.

Christopher rose, too.

"So do I," he told them. He was in tears. "You are disgusting and ugly, both of you!"

Instead of going to his own room, he followed his sister into hers.

Natalie was left alone at the top of the stairs. Her little face crumpled.

After the first split second of shock, Miranda leaped towards her, to take her baby in her arms, and comfort her. But just as she came close, Christopher rushed out of Lydia's bedroom and, pushing Miranda roughly aside, snatched Natalie up in his arms.

"Go on with your filthy quarrel!" he screamed. "Leave poor Natty *alone!*"

He carried her, weeping, through the door, and banged it behind him with such force that the doorknob spun off and rolled across the carpet.

Miranda was deeply, deeply shaken. She sank toward the floor, like a doll without stuffing. Her knees were trembling visibly. Her hands were shaking. Even her mouth was quivering horribly. Daniel felt terrible.

"Miranda —"

"Get out of this house."

"Miranda, *please!*"

"I want you to *go.*"

Daniel looked down at the doorknob on the carpet.

"What about the children?" he asked. "Should I take them with me? Today is Tuesday, after all . . ."

His voice faded away. And there was no standing up against the look she turned on him.

Hurrying past her with his own knees shaking, Daniel went into the large double bedroom to fetch the clothing he had left there. It lay in a sordid little heap on the floor. He looked, and felt sickened. But there was nothing else to wear. What he'd not taken with him when he left, Miranda had given to the Goodwill years ago.

As he arranged himself as Madame Doubtfire one last time, he wondered whether he might not put right some of the damage done. Instead of just walking past her on his way out, he could sit down beside her on the stairs, perhaps slip a comforting arm around her shoulders, offer her one of her own drinks, try and thrash things out.

But it wouldn't work. The day of the storm is not a day for thatching. It wouldn't work.

When he came out, she had not moved. She sat like cold stone as he picked his way past her and down the stairs. He lifted his turban from where it lay on the floor and rammed it fiercely on his head as he went out of the front door.

Mrs. Hooper, he noticed, was leaning dangerously far over the fence, still eavesdropping in hopes of hearing more.

He said to her spitefully, as he left:

"I see your giant hogweed's coming up nice and early."

Even her crushed expression failed to console him.

10

The Looking Glass River

Daniel didn't wait at the bus stop. Given the circumstances he hardly felt like standing, still dressed as Madame Doubtfire, in full view of Mrs. Hooper watching him from her garden, and his own children staring down from Lydia's bedroom, and possibly even Miranda glowering at him through a downstairs window. Instead, he strode off down the road, and slowed his pace only after turning the corner.

Several streets on, he heard a bus approaching from behind and stuck out his hand as he kept walking, indifferent in his misery as to whether or not the driver bothered to stop for him. The bus did draw up, though, and Daniel stepped aboard. Only as the driver let out the clutch and traveled on toward the next real stop did Daniel realize that he had no bus fare.

"Dear me! It seems I've left my handbag behind!"

Daniel had asked for and taken his ticket gruffly enough; but now that he realized he couldn't pay for it, out of instinctive prudence he made some effort to allay the driver's wrath by using Madame Doubtfire as a shield.

"Oh, what a silly billy I am! How irritating for you, driver. After you've dealt out the ticket, too! Oh, I am sorry."

The driver was entirely mollified. Indeed, he seemed to find Madame Doubtfire quite charming.

"Never you mind, ma'am. Have this ride on me. You sit down. Rest your weary legs."

"It's terribly good of you," warbled Daniel. "You are too kind, too kind."

Blushing, the driver motioned to Madame Doubtfire to be companionable and take the closest seat reserved for the infirm or elderly, so he could carry on the conversation. Daniel was far too distracted to think to refuse. He perched tensely on the very edge of his seat, plucking nervously at his skirt, and nodding automatically at anything the driver said. His mind was fully taken up with a vivid and searing inner review of his appalling quarrel with Miranda, and with seeing over again in his mind's eye the strain and distress on his children's faces.

A good few bus stops had flown by before Daniel surfaced sufficiently from his wretchedness to realize the driver was no longer simply being friendly: he had moved on to unabashed flirtation.

Daniel cursed Madame Doubtfire for a witch.

"My stop!" he trilled.

"Can't stop till after the rotary, love."

The driver continued his series of heavy hints about lonely weekends.

Involuntarily, Daniel blushed.

The driver seemed to find this most becoming. He leered at Madame Doubtfire with undisguised enthusiasm. Already overwrought, Daniel now panicked. He felt trapped, and all hot and bothered. Without a thought, he started rolling up his sleeves. But before he'd so much as turned each pretty frilled cuff back on itself a couple of times, the driver had suddenly returned his attention to the traffic, and was staring quite fixedly at the road ahead.

Lowering his head with relief, Daniel noticed for the first time his own arms lying in his lap — huge, sturdy, muscle-knotted arms, crawling all over with thick black hairs.

Surreptitiously, Daniel peeped at the driver. Unfortunately their eyes fleetingly met in one of the circular mirrors. The driver looked away at once, nervous and embarrassed, recalling all the neglected friends he really should try to make time to see over the weekend. At the next intersection, Daniel leaped off.

The first thing Daniel did when he reached home was rip off his turban and frock, and stuff everything that belonged to Madame Doubtfire into a huge black plastic sack and carry it down to the garbage cans. "Good riddance!" he shouted, stuffing the bag down among the chicken bones and tea leaves and carrot peelings. "Goodbye, turbans! Farewell, lavender water! Adieu, *Apricot Crême* Foundation! Good riddance to you, Madame Doubtfire! Thank God we'll never meet again!"

Then he kicked the garbage can hard, once, for good measure.

The next thing he did was raid the cracked teapot in which he kept his emergency money. There was six pounds. With this, Daniel rushed out and bought himself a mop, a scrubbing brush, two packs of cloths, and three tubs of abrasive cleaning powder. Messy and squalid, she had called his flat. He'd show Miranda! She would see!

He swept the floor, and mopped it till it gleamed. He tried to add color to the task by imagining that there had been some terrible household accident and he was mopping up Miranda's blood, but for once his heart wasn't in it, somehow. Perhaps he felt just a little too guilty. Some of the things she'd said to him had really hit home.

As soon as the floor was spotless, he started on the oven. Miranda had been quite right to wrinkle up her nose at it, he decided. It was disgusting. He had to scrape off the top few layers of grease with a knife, wiping the blade on newspaper time and again. Now that he was actually dabbling his fingers in the squalor, as it were, he saw for the first time how very nasty it could be, and he bitterly regretted having allowed his new home to become so unsavory and unhygienic. Certain old memories swam in his mind as he scoured and scrubbed, and he remembered in particular an occasion on which he had offered to let Lydia hold her birthday party in his apartment after Miranda had put her foot down, saying that birthday parties had to stop some time, and this year was as good as any.

Lydia hadn't simply refused his offer. She had shuddered. He'd seen her, distinctly. It was the reason he remembered the occasion so clearly. And though, at the time, he'd taken her polite refusal at its face value, and put all other possible reasons firmly from mind, now, looking back, he realized why she had inadvertently looked so horrified at the suggestion, and he felt the same deep embarrassment at having even offered his grubby and unappealing hospitality to her schoolfriends as she must have felt on imagining its acceptance.

Dust is dust. Grime is grime. But filth is filth. Daniel threw himself with renewed fervor into the battle, and this battle was against King Filth himself. The sink was glistening in the sunlight that poured through the freshly polished windowpanes when the doorbell rang.

Daniel's hands were impacted with cleaning powder. He walked down the hall and lifted the latch with his elbow.

His elder daughter stood outside. She was, he realized in astonishment, wearing a heavy winter coat — the one he'd bought her last year, and hadn't seen since.

"Lydia! You've come!"

"Yes. Here I am."

She didn't sound at all pleased about it.

Daniel stepped back to let her pass.

"Can I make you some tea?"

"No, thank you."

Her tone was chilly, and her manner unfriendly. She walked straight past the kitchen without so much as a glance inside to see all his lovely, sparkling surfaces. She plonked herself unceremoniously down in front of the television, and scowled at the blank screen.

After a moment, Daniel ventured:

"That was a doozy and a half between me and your mother . . ."

"It was horrible. *Horrible.*"

"Not the occasion for the committed pacifist, it must be admitted."

"You were both *very nasty indeed.*"

Daniel disguised his embarrassment by moving around the room picking up old newspapers. He thrust them into the wastebasket. Every now and again, he came upon an odd sock, and slipped it gratefully into his pocket. The straying socks of children of divorce, he thought, were very possibly the twentieth-century equivalent of all those olive branches of biblical times.

Lydia still sat scowling at the empty screen. Daniel was finding it most unnerving. He tried again.

"Oh, it was nasty. Constructive criticism, now, I can accept; but as for simple abuse —"

"Listen," Lydia interrupted him very coldly indeed. "I don't really want to talk, if you don't mind. Or listen, either. And I certainly don't want to talk about *that.*"

"Why are you here, then?" Daniel asked, astonished.

Two tiny spots of red appeared on the ridge of Lydia's cheekbones.

"Because it's Tuesday teatime," she said.

"And Tuesday teatime is *my* time?"

The scowl was deepening.

"It's just the principle of the thing," she said.

"You're simply exerting what you see as your rights?"

"You could say that. I'm certainly not expecting to have a good time!"

"I'll make tea anyway," Daniel said hastily, and backed away into the kitchen. He put the kettle on, and while he waited for the water to boil, he scrubbed out the small space between the fridge and the vegetable rack from which he'd taken his wooden tea tray. In there, to his deep mortification, Daniel discovered two more socks.

When he returned a few minutes later, carrying the tray, Lydia was feeling a bit more forthcoming. And as the tea and biscuits filled her, her voice warmed up.

"It isn't *just* the principle of the thing," she confided after a while. "There's something else as well."

"Oh, yes?"

"Something I thought about before a little, when Mother was telling us about your wedding. I thought then that, if either of you two had backed out, none of us children would ever have been born."

"But you *were* born."

"Yes. And that's the point. We were born. And we're the only things that lasted, aren't we? I mean, the marriage was a failure. A total failure. And you two aren't really even friends anymore." She shook her head impatiently, looking, Daniel thought, more like her mother than he'd ever seen her. "Oh, I know you make a pretty good show of getting along well when you bump into one another at other people's parties, or at school evenings, and things like that. But you're not really good *friends* anymore, are you?"

"No," Daniel admitted. "We're not really good friends."

"So, I was thinking, Natty and Christopher and

me, we are the only three things to come out of that marriage. We're all that's left. We're the whole *point,* now."

"The whole point?"

His voice was gentle, if a little mystified.

"Yes. The whole point. The only reason you two have any real contact. So that gives us a sort of Extra Right. Don't you see? Don't you *see?* If we three are not happy with the way things are, then what was the point of all those years? None! None at all! If you can't work things out to suit *us,* then all it was was total waste and total failure. In fact —" she hesitated. "*Worse* than just total waste and failure."

"Worse?"

"Yes. Worse. Hatred and arguments and all that ugly, ugly stuff."

"Oh, yes," said Daniel. "Ugly stuff." He paused, remembering. Then he asked: "Did you tell *her* this?"

"No. No, I didn't. I would have tried, but she wasn't listening. She was too angry and upset."

"With me."

"And me." She rose, and moved across to the window and stared out, her hands thrust deep down in the pockets of her winter coat. It didn't really suit her, Daniel decided. The pattern was too strong, and it made her look frumpish. She looked much nicer in the one Miranda bought.

"How did you get here?" he asked her.

"I had a fight. She didn't want me to come. She called me disloyal. She said you'd forfeited your right to a visit today."

"What did you say?"

Lydia turned. Her eyes were filled with tears. She looked exhausted.

"I told her I was not going to live my life between the two of you any more, thinking about her rights and yours. I told her I thought I had rights of my *own*, and from now on you two had better start thinking of *mine*."

Daniel's eyes widened.

"What did she say when you said that?"

"I didn't actually *say* it," confessed Lydia. "I *yelled* it."

"And she said —?"

"Yelled."

"Yelled —?"

"That I couldn't go. That I was in too much of a state!"

"And you said —"

"Yelled. I yelled that . . ." She hesitated. Her voice was shaking at the memory. "I yelled at her that, if she didn't let me go today, she would regret it!"

"Regret it?"

"Yes."

Daniel looked thoughtful.

"What did you have in mind, exactly, when you told her that?"

Lydia turned back to the window.

"I'm not quite sure," she told him. "I'm not quite sure. But she should know — it's time she knew — that you can order someone around and still not win. You can control them, and still lose them. If she would only stop and *think*, she'd realize that."

"Oh, yes," said Daniel. "And when she stops and thinks, she's going to realize that. Don't you worry."

Lydia sighed. Shutting her eyes, she lifted a hand to rub the skin between her eyes.

"And then I just went down to the basement and fetched this coat, and then I walked outside and caught the first bus into the center of town."

"And came here on your own steam."

"It took a bit of time. But I did it." She blushed a little. "Though I did forget my bus fare. My purse was in the other coat, you see. I never thought. The driver was so nice, though. He let me on without the fare. He said I wasn't the first person to forget her money today, either. He said some senile old lady did exactly the same, this very afternoon, on the same route."

"Senile old lady?" Daniel was momentarily outraged on the late Madame Doubtfire's behalf. "*Senile old lady?*"

Then he stood up, and walked over to his daughter's side. Gently, he slid the hideous, bulky winter coat off her shoulders.

"You look worn out," he told her as he steered

her toward the sofa. "Why don't you have a little rest?"

"I could," she confessed. "I'm very tired. I'm so tired I could sleep through vacuuming."

He left the room and, pulling the door closed behind him, dialed Miranda's number. There was no answer.

When he came back with the blankets, her eyes were closed.

She did sleep through the vacuuming. And she slept through the wiping of the kitchen cabinets, and the polishing of the mirrors. She slept through the emptying of the wastebaskets and the fixing of the bookshelf. She slept through the straightening of the window blinds.

Then Natalie woke her up, by bursting through the front door clutching a large plastic bag to her stomach, and rushing through the apartment poking her head into each room, and shouting:

"Dadd — *eee!*"

Daniel emerged from his freshly gleaming bathroom.

"Surprise, surprise!" he exclaimed. "And is Christopher with you?"

"He's coming up, with Mother."

Miranda and Christopher appeared together in the doorway. Christopher looked quite himself again — indeed, he looked almost merry — but Miranda's eyes were red-rimmed, and her face was still pale.

Daniel and Miranda eyed one another nervously.

"Hello, Dan."

"Hello there, Miranda." He searched for words. "It's nice of you to drive them over here, considering . . ."

"Well," she said, embarrassed. "It *is* Tuesday." She still looked very shaken, he decided. "And they insisted."

"Nonetheless," Daniel said. "Given the circumstances . . ."

And they both blushed.

"Please," Daniel begged her. "Stay for a quick cup of tea. You look so white. I don't like to think of you driving back just yet."

"Well —" She was doubtful. "I don't know . . ."

"Yes," Christopher ordered. "You look as though you've been put through the wringer. Stay and have one nice cup of tea, with Dad."

"Oh, I —"

"Good!" Daniel said. "Splendid. Come on in."

On the way into the kitchen he flapped his arms in a desperate fashion at Christopher, behind her back, signaling his son to herd Natalie away, and keep Lydia out, and leave the two of them in peace. With the most haughty expression he could muster, Christopher cooperated. He found his father's frantic dumbshow insulting and demeaning. Leaving both parents alone together was what he had intended all the time.

Miranda tried to disguise her initial unease by admiring his cleaning efforts.

"You've done so much! It looks a lot better. I'm sorry if I was rude about your apartment, but it had got in such a *state*."

"You were quite right," Daniel assured her. "It was disgusting."

Miranda's eyes touched lightly on the shears, still sitting open-jawed on the stool.

"May I?" she asked politely.

She lifted them off, snapped the blades shut, and tipped them more safely, points down, in the corner.

"*Please,*" Daniel reassured her. "Please do. I think I need all the help I can get."

Miranda sighed.

"Maybe we both do." She passed him the tea caddy, and stood beside him as he warmed the pot. "Not that I'm suggesting for a single moment that I want Madame Doubtfire back!"

"She's dead," Daniel informed her. He looked out of the window. The garbage cans had been emptied. "She's dead and gone."

"Well, I'm not sorry."

"Neither am I." He lowered his head, pouring the boiling water on the tea leaves. "But I am sorry that we all deceived you. It was a rotten thing to do."

"Maybe I should have been a bit more reasonable." She waved her hands around. "But really, you see, I didn't want them here. Not with . . ." Her voice trailed away. Her eyes touched lightly on the safely placed shears, and came to rest on his frayed electrical wire.

"No, I understand," Daniel said. "It was disgusting, and parts of it were actually unsafe. But now that I'm getting more organized, a lot of things are going to change around here, and if you see anything that makes you nervous, you let me know, and I'll do what I can."

"Thank you," she said. "Thank you."

He handed her a cup of tea. She took a sip.

"Good," she said. "But not as good as Madame Doubtfire's tea."

"You," Daniel said just a little bit stiffly, "can afford to buy much better tea than I can."

Miranda was looking embarrassed again.

"Listen, Daniel," she said. "I'll be quite frank with you. I don't want you back as a housekeeper, even as yourself. I know you did a good job; but I don't want you. I can't explain it. It's just how I feel. But maybe we could manage some sort of a compromise here. How would you like to earn a bit of money taking a job as my gardener? When it rains, you could let yourself into the house and make a pot of coffee and care for the plants inside. And if you worked in the late afternoons, you'd get to see the children, too."

She paused, and went bright red.

"After all," she told him. "You are their father."

It didn't take him any time at all to decide.

"You're *on!*" he said, delighted. "Though I might dig my trench for the potatoes a little deeper than usual for the first couple of years, in case of sniping from the house." He dug into his pockets. "Here. Take these as a small token of my good faith and gratitude."

Into her hand he thrust a dozen odd socks.

"Oh, Daniel!"

She was plainly moved as she shoveled the socks in her handbag. Daniel felt close to tears himself.

"*And* I won't phone at mealtimes anymore."

"And I'll stop getting irritable whenever you're mentioned."

They smiled at each other.

"Shake hands," he said.

And they shook hands.

"I won't drive back and fetch them," she told him. "Unless they particularly want to come home. They can sleep over here, if that suits you, because they're on strike still tomorrow, and I am going to need your help in any case. I have to leave for Matlock first thing in the morning."

"I'll have them home when you get back."

"Thanks, Dan."

She leaned across, and kissed him lightly on the cheek.

"Thanks, Dan," she said again, and hurried out.

Daniel was still nursing his kiss with the palm of his hand when Christopher emerged.

"Well," Christopher said, rubbing his hands together with satisfaction. "That went well."

"Were you *listening*?"

"Only a little. Not a lot."

"You've got a nerve," said Daniel. "It's none of your business."

"None of my business?" Christopher was outraged. "Who do you think it was who got her to come here? Who do you think it was who went *on* and *on* at her, and wouldn't do anything else, and wouldn't drop the topic, and just kept saying *over* and *over* again that it was Tuesday and we wanted to come here? Me and Natty! That's who!"

"I'm very grateful," said Daniel. "It went well."

"I knew it would."

"Oh, *you*," Daniel told him loftily. "You're a *child*. It is a well-known fact that children have in their nature an almost unlimited capacity for optimism and forgiveness."

"Lucky for you two!" scoffed Christopher.

"Too right," agreed Daniel. He, for one, was sincerely grateful.

In the living room, Natty was waiting for him.

She bounced up and down with excitement on the sofa, still clutching her precious plastic bag.

"What have you got in there, then?" asked Daniel.

Proudly, very proudly, she drew out her most precious possession. It was the picture book — *The Looking Glass River*.

"I'm going to keep it here now," she announced gravely. "Here in this home."

"You picked a good day to make this decision, Natalie," Daniel informed his daughter with equal gravity. "I fixed the bookshelf only this afternoon."

He sat on the sofa between Natalie and Lydia.

"You can sleep over," he said. "Do you want to?"

"Yes," Christopher said promptly. "You bet."

Lydia considered a moment.

"I *think* I'll stay," she said, pulling the blankets up to her chin. "Yes, I think so. But tell her I'll be happy to come home if she changes her mind."

"I'll stay," said Natalie. "If Lydia stays."

"Right, then," said Daniel, reaching out for the book. "*The Looking Glass River.*" Natalie crawled on to his knee and Christopher took her space, and sat fiddling quietly with his calculator, pretending not to listen. Lydia unashamedly snuggled further down under her blankets to enjoy the old story.

"*Hundreds of people have searched for the Looking Glass River,*" Daniel began to read. "*Its waters are —*"

Outside, in the hall, the phone began to ring. The children tensed.

"I'll get it!" Daniel cried, and leaped to his feet. He strode across the room and out, banging the door behind him. He lifted the receiver. Yes, it was Miranda.

"Yes?" he said warily. "Do you want them back?"

"Oh, no!" She brushed the very suggestion aside. "Oh, Daniel. I've just got home, and —"

His voice warmed up.

"What? Tell me, Miranda. What's the matter?"

"It's Hetty. I just walked in, and she's lying in her cage and her feet are —" She stopped, and finished up: "Well, she's *dead*."

"I'm sorry," Daniel said. "Was it a shock?"

"No," said Miranda. "But it is a *nuisance*."

Down the line, Daniel could hear her sighing.

"Daniel, will you do me a favor? Please? Will you tell them? I mean, you know me." She sighed again. "I'm just no good at telling them this sort of thing. I get impatient with all their tears and messy grave-markers and stuff. I mean, when all's said and done, a quail's just a quail. And she was *ancient*."

Daniel looked up to the ceiling, and grinned.

"Good old Miranda!" he said, remembering with sudden force why he proposed to her in the first place all those years ago. "That's my girl!"

"I beg your pardon?"

"Nothing. I mean, you're dead right. A quail's just a quail."

"But not to Christopher."

"No, not to him."

"So will you tell him? Please? You're so much better than I am at that sort of thing."

"I'll tell him," Daniel said. "I'll tell him tomorrow."

"I think that's best. Leave it until tomorrow. We've all had quite enough today."

"I won't forget." He shifted his weight. "Now listen, Miranda. You've got a long drive ahead of you tomorrow. Just spread an old towel over the cage, and put it in the basement, and forget it. I'll sort the whole business out tomorrow."

"Right." There was a pause, then: "Are they staying?"

"Yes," Daniel told her. "Lydia was a little dubious. I think she rather wanted to be with you tonight."

"Oh!"

She sounded pleased, and a little relieved.

"But she's a bit wiped out, so in the end she thought she'd stay, unless you change your mind and want her back."

"No, I won't change my mind. I thought I'd just have one quick drink with Sam, and then a really early night."

"That worked out well, then," said Daniel. "You won't need a sitter."

"And you won't be alone, after the sad demise of your friend Madame Doubtfire."

Both of them hung up laughing.

The children saw him walk in with the smile still on his face.

"Who was that?"

"Your mother."

"Really? What did she want?"

"Just chatting," Daniel said. "Nothing that won't wait. Where were we in the story, Natty?"

She made him start all over again. He opened the book at the beginning. There was the river, flowing in cool blue and green across the first page. Gracefully, the willow trees leaned over their own reflections. The little cottages along its banks stood out in fresh, bright colors. In the clear skies overhead, swallows wheeled.

"*Hundreds of people have searched for the Looking Glass River,*" read Daniel. "*Its waters are calm and still as glass. Anyone who drinks of its waters feels at peace. There are no quarrels in the families who live beside Looking Glass River . . .*"

He didn't need to read it to keep going. He knew the whole story by heart. He raised his eyes for a moment, and saw his two elder children grinning at each other.

His youngest child just squeezed his hand.